THE TRAILSMAN 25

MAVERICK MAIDEN

by
Jon Sharpe

D1560311

A SIGNET BOOK
NEW AMERICAN LIBRARY

PUBLISHER'S NOTE

This novel is a work of fiction. Names, characters, places, and incidents either are the product of the author's imagination or are used fictitiously, and any resemblance to actual persons, living or dead, events, or locales is entirely coincidental.

NAL BOOKS ARE AVAILABLE AT QUANTITY DISCOUNTS
WHEN USED TO PROMOTE PRODUCTS OR SERVICES.
FOR INFORMATION PLEASE WRITE TO PREMIUM MARKETING DIVISION,
THE NEW AMERICAN LIBRARY, INC., 1633 BROADWAY,
NEW YORK, NEW YORK 10019.

The first chapter of this book appeared in *Twisted Noose*, the twenty-fourth volume in this series.

SIGNET TRADEMARK REG. U.S. PAT. OFF. AND FOREIGN COUNTRIES
REGISTERED TRADEMARK—MARCA REGISTRADA
HECHO EN CHICAGO, U.S.A.

SIGNET, SIGNET CLASSIC, MENTOR, PLUME, MERIDIAN AND NAL BOOKS
are published by The New American Library, Inc.,
1633 Broadway, New York, New York 10019

First Printing, January, 1984

1 2 3 4 5 6 7 8 9

PRINTED IN THE UNITED STATES OF AMERICA

The Trailsman

Beginnings . . . they bend the tree and they
mark the man. Skye Fargo was born when
he was eighteen. Terror was his midwife,
vengeance his first cry. Killing spawned
Skye Fargo, ruthless, cold-blooded murder.
Out of the acrid smoke of gunpowder
still hanging in the air, he rose, cried
out a promise never forgotten.

The Trailsman, they began to call him
all across the West: searcher, scout,
hunter, the man who could see where
others only looked, his skills for hire but
not his soul, the man who lived each day
to the fullest, yet trailed each tomorrow.
Skye Fargo, the Trailsman, the seeker
who could take the wildness of a land and
the wanting of a woman and make them
his own.

*A sizzling summer in early Texas,
when the guns in the territory
turned as hot as hell itself . . .*

1

Fargo scuttled over the sharp, jagged rock to the smooth shoulder high on the side of the gorge. From here he could see the top of the grizzled rocks, and his gun was out, ready to blow the head off this mystery, mangy, sneaky gunman who'd been trying to potshot him for the last two days. He shot always from high ground and then moved like greased lightning. By the time Fargo made the climb, his target skidded into thin air—like now.

The sun on this side of the gorge hit down like a hammer, and Fargo mopped the sweat off his bronzed square face. His piercing lake-blue eyes raked every inch of the rocks, searching for a move, while his ears strained for sound.

Suddenly an alarm did go off, for he heard sound, but it came not from the gorge but from the canyon. Two men were on horses, skulking behind the boulders that bordered the trail. They were waiting, and from Fargo's perch, he could see clearly enough what they waited for—a short-haul Texas wagon with its driver and four passengers running easy for Eagle Butte. Running, Fargo thought, right into ambush.

Fargo felt a jolt of anger at the cards being dealt him. First, he was trying to get to Red Clay to track down a lead in his quest for revenge. Second, he'd been sidetracked by this mystery bushwhacker, who, for no damned logical reason, had been throwing lead at him. Now he was about to be pushed into the cross fire of a trailway robbery.

He gritted his teeth, and for a closer look at the gunmen, moved with catlike step down over the scarred iron-colored rocks. Now he had a sharper view and he stared hard at the two men, now with guns drawn. They were both stubble-bearded, short, muscular, with the same body stamp, except one was a bit leaner, taller. They wore black hats, black vests, red kerchiefs. As Fargo studied them the short one spoke and the lean one laughed, an ugly hard laugh. The kind of laugh that triggered a memory of men he often seemed to meet in the territory, men of evil. He thought of his dead family and felt a surge of hate and moved down, quiet and fast. The gunmen were unaware of him, but on the other hand, they were out of his rifle range. To be helpful to the passengers in that wagon, he knew he should get into the action plenty fast. It was a Texas cotton-bed wagon, with its top sawed off, used for short hauls.

He shot a glance at the driver, big-shouldered, big hat, riding easy, blissfully ignorant that behind the curve in the trail he was headed right into a trap. Fargo felt his breathing come quicker and cursed softly. Then, as the driver slowed his team because of the curve, the two gunmen moved out, blocking the trail. Startled at the sight ahead of him, the driver pulled hard on the reins and the horses came to a halt, snorting and stomping.

"What the hell," the driver said, slowly raising his hands.

The short man shot him anyway, quickly, as if the idea had already been in his head. The big driver grabbed at his chest, then cursed as he pitched facedown to the ground.

Fargo's jaw hardened and he measured the distance —still out of range. He moved faster, silently, from boulder to boulder. He had an ugly foreboding.

The gunmen swung off their horses with guns pointing and yelled hard at the passengers. They came down slowly, two portly men in vested suits, a dude in black eastern suit, a buxom, brown-haired girl in a blue cotton dress. They looked at the bleeding body of the driver, then stared in fear at the gunmen.

"Throw your money here," the short man yelled, waving his gun, while the lean gunman bit into a wad of tobacco. The portly men hurriedly pulled their wallets and tossed them. The dude was scowling, his pale face twisted with disbelief—he couldn't understand the violence. "Are you men crazy? You can't get away with this!"

The lean man had bent to pick up a wallet, but at the words he froze, then shot the dude in the heart. The bullet flung him back as if he'd been hit by a hammer and he sat down, his eyes like saucers, staring. Slowly he put his hand to his bloody chest, stared at it, amazed, looked at the gunman, then slid down to the earth.

The short man glared at the lean man, shook his head. "That was stupid, Luke. Now we gotta be mean." And he shot the other two men, and when they fell squirming to the ground, he shot them again.

Fargo cursed; it had been too quick, and he had made a mistake. If he had fired, even if his bullets fell short, it might have saved the men by distracting the gunmen.

These were killers without mercy, he hadn't ex-

11

pected that. They had killed to eliminate witnesses, and now he feared for the girl. After they pleasured themselves with her, there'd be no telling what might happen. He had to move fast.

The girl, horrified by the killings, panicked and began to run. "Grab her, Shorty." Luke smirked. Shorty laughed, made a sprinting tackle and brought her down. As he rolled over her, contact with her body seemed to trigger his desires, and he began to pull at her dress. A rip brought out her breasts and the sight of them made him whistle.

"Hey, Luke," he called. "Lookit this piece. Ever see such tits?"

Luke's mind seemed to be on money, for he kept picking the pockets of the men and looking into the wallets.

Shorty tried to get the girl's dress up, but she fought him, and furious, he ripped it completely off her body, pulling and tearing until she was absolutely nude. "Hey, Luke, forget the money. Look at this. It's cherry, I'll bet, and best there is."

The girl had full breasts, full hips, a well-shaped body. She squirmed so hard that Shorty, who had opened his breeches, couldn't make headway. "C'mere, Luke, hold her hands," he yelled. "I'm going to nail this hellcat."

Luke came over, and by this time Fargo felt he had picked up range. Maybe it'd been a good idea anyway to wait until the men were near each other. Luke had grabbed the girl's hands, and Shorty was trying to get between the girl's thighs, but she squirmed and twisted, and Shorty, in a fury of frustration, swung at the girl, knocking her flat. He stood and looked at her, scowling. For a moment she lay stunned, then slowly got up and faced him, a red bruise on her cheek.

12

Shorty took his gun from its holster, unbuttoned his belt, let his breeches drop to his ankles. His organ was in a state of real excitement. Deliberately he shot a bullet at her feet, raising dust. "I'm tired of rassling you, you lil' bitch. Now I'll give you just one minute to come over here and make love to this thing or I'll put a bullet in your bush."

The words floated clearly up to Fargo and his face reddened with anger.

The girl looked at Shorty's erection with revulsion, and though in fear, she lifted her head. "Shoot, you skunk, because I'd rather die."

Shorty, his face hard, threatening, slowly raised his gun.

Now Fargo had him in sight and squeezed the trigger. Shorty shrieked and looked down. Only a bleeding stump was left of his sex organ. He skrieked again and again in pain, in anguish, in horror.

Luke stared at him in shock, then pulled his gun, searching for the gunman in the high rocks, but the next bullet hit his own right eye, blasting it, and with it, part of his skull. He fell like an axed tree.

The girl looked as if a thunderbolt from heaven had saved her, and her eyes, scanning the rocks, saw the lean, square-faced man with the rifle, now coming toward her.

Shorty was staring at Luke, then looked down to see the blood of his life pumping out of his groin. He fell to his knees, his face grimacing horribly, and struggled to raise his gun to fire at the lean rifleman coming toward him. The rifle shot echoed in the gorge and a hole appeared in Shorty's head as his brains spurted into the air and he fell forward, facedown.

The girl screamed, covered her eyes, grabbed her clothing and ran behind a rock.

"Nothing more to worry about, miss," Fargo said quietly.

He looked down at Luke, who was not a pretty sight, his pockets bulging with stolen wallets. "No point in wasting this," he said. He put the booty all together into a red neckerchief and then looked at the young woman coming from behind the rock. The rips in the dress she wore still revealed parts of her body. She was a pretty thing, he thought, a pert face, dark brown eyes, a sweet mouth, and she was certainly gutsy.

"They were no gentlemen." His voice was ironic.

"They were animals . . . worse!" She bit her lip. "I don't know how to thank you."

He stared at the men so quiet in death, their evil brought to a violent standstill. "Don't thank me. It's a pleasure to wipe such men from the face of the earth." He turned. "Where you headed, miss?"

"My name is Amy Jackson. I was headed for Eagle Butte."

"Just get up on that black horse, Miss Jackson. I'll give you escort."

A quiver of anxiety flashed in her face, as if she were wondering if he were a man to be trusted. He'd seen her naked, after all. Fargo understood her concern. "My name is Skye Fargo. I don't think you need worry too much from now on."

He sounded right, and suddenly reassured, she flashed him a look of gratitude and swung over the black's saddle.

When they reached Eagle Butte, a small worried group had collected at the depot with its painted sign: Short Haul Line. A gray-haired, pink-faced lady in the group waved at sight of Amy. The others looked shocked as they observed the state of her clothes, the bruise on her face.

14

"My god, Amy, what happened?" the lady cried.

Amy dismounted and they crowded around while the girl told the details, not sparing any of the horror of the holdup and massacre, and particularly Fargo's sharpshooting.

The listeners were shocked at the brutal killings. "It was those mean Jones boys," a hard-faced cowboy said. One heavy-set man in a brown Stetson stared with hostile eyes at Fargo. "Why didn't you shoot the moment you saw the holdup, mister? Why'd you wait?"

Fargo grimaced. "I was out of range. And thought it'd just be a robbery, that I'd have time. Men don't kill so easy for money."

"These men do," said the cowboy. "The Jones boys, Shorty and Luke. Wanted for killings all over the territory."

Fargo stroked his cheek. "I suppose I should have fired, even out of range. It might have stopped them. It was a mistake."

"You made a mistake, mister, and my cousin is dead," said the heavy-set man.

"It's very sad that you lost your cousin, Clem," said Mrs. Jackson. "But the killers are dead. And Amy is alive and unhurt because of Mr. Fargo. I think instead of blaming him, we owe him thanks."

The other people nodded, and one man grunted. "Got rid of two of the worst killers in the county."

Fargo nodded and smiled at Amy, who flashed him a warm, grateful look. He walked down the dirt street lined with white or unpainted wooden buildings; a livery shop, a general merchandise store, Mama Joy's Café, a saloon and Brown's Hotel. Two crusty buildings that looked abandoned brought up the end of the street.

Fargo took a room at the hotel for the night,

15

washed his grimy face in a basin of hot water, sprawled on the bed for an hour, basking in its soft luxury. Then he went out, down the street and toward Miller's Saloon.

The saloon was surprisingly big, a long bar, with a mirror behind it, several drinkers, two tables with card players and a battered piano played by a sad-faced black man. Three women in low-cut red dresses and spangled jewelry, laughing, were in the back, near stairs that obviously went up to private rooms.

The barman, Miller, came up, a man with a red face, big red nose, shrewd brown eyes.

"Whiskey," Fargo said.

The barman poured a drink, studied Fargo a moment, then smiled. He set up another glass, filled it. "Have one on the house, mister." He smiled.

"Why?"

"You're Fargo, right? We heard about the stage-coach. And we heard too about Shorty Jones. What you did." He grinned. "You shortened him a bit, I heard. And you shot from up in the hills. Must have an eye like an eagle."

Fargo picked up his glass. "Thanks for the drink." When the barman went off to attend another customer, Fargo looked into the mirror. He could see the women clearly enough and found it pleasing to look at one of them, a redhead with a pretty face, surprisingly abundant breasts in a slender, well-shaped body. She wore a red silklike dress, tight against her figure, its low cut showing a fine pair of deep breasts. She couldn't be more than twenty, and her face had the kind of innocence that would always be there, whatever way she lived. She seemed busy laughing at a story told by one of the women.

Just then one of the men from the bar came over, bent low and whispered in her ear; whatever it was, it hit her hard, for she turned sharply to look right at the reflection in the mirror. With the quickness of a clever woman, she moved in on Fargo's interest, smiled brightly. Then she walked to an empty table, sat down and crooked her finger at him, which made him smile. She had no doubt he'd come over. She was a damned pretty thing, could fascinate any man who appealed to her, and for one moment he was tempted to throw a block, stay put and see how she handled it. Then decided against it. He hadn't had a woman for weeks, and his groin was in an uproar, specially after the sight of Amy, all nude and luscious out on the trail. He couldn't very well tackle Amy after her scary experience with the Jones boys, but this girl, bold, deep-chested, young for a party girl, looked irresistible to him. So he took his glass and ambled over to her table.

For some reason, the pianist at that moment decided to play, and it was a romantic, pretty tune that sounded just fine for his intentions.

"Did you invite me?" he asked.

"Oh yes. You *are* Fargo, aren't you?"

He nodded, surprised, and sat down. Close up, she had a fine aquiline nose, a wide-lipped mouth and gray eyes. Her red hair curled pleasingly around her face, which had a few freckles, and the white bulge of her breasts made him feel hornier than ever.

"I'm Fargo."

"I'm Mady," she said. "And I want to thank you for ridding the world of a sewer rat."

His eyebrows went up. "Who would that be?"

"Shorty Jones, that's who it would be." Her eyes flashed fire. "The rottenest rat that ever lived."

17

He lifted his glass. "It sounds personal."

"It's personal, all right!" Her eyes suddenly filled with tears. "He shot and killed my father two years ago. In Glen Rose, where we had a general store. Came in one day for bullets, he was all out. When my father asked for money, he said, 'You got it all wrong, mister. It's you who pays the money.' And he pointed the gun at Dad. 'That's a lowdown trick,' Dad says. I was in the store at the time. 'I'm sorry you don't like my manners,' said Shorty, 'but I don't like to be cussed.' Then he shot Daddy, just like that, two bullets. Paralyzed him. Then Shorty grabbed the money in the drawer, said he was sorry he didn't have time for me just then and raced off, to his brother, standing watch outside. These Jones boys were the worst in the territory. And I heard the way you did Shorty in. Everyone in town's heard it. We ought to give you a medal." She leaned forward, put her soft fingers on his face and planted a warm kiss on his lips.

He grinned, pulled a cheroot, scratched the match on his jeans. "I'm glad to avenge your daddy. The truth is, I hate scum like that wherever I see it. And I try to do my bit to clean up the territory, if I can."

She was looking at his dusty clothes. "You been riding long, haven't you? Where you headed?"

"Trying to nail two more sewer rats."

"If you're not in a hurry, maybe you could stop for a bath." Her eyes fixed on his, and her full lips smiled meaningfully. "You might want to ease up some. A man needs to ease up."

He felt a hardening in his breeches, and Mady, with the instinct of a woman who knew when such things happen, suddenly smiled.

He followed her upstairs to a spacious room that

18

looked very feminine, with frilly curtains on the window, a cloth on the bureau, a red coverlet on the large bed. He sat on the bed testing its softness. "This feels good," he said.

She was standing in front of him, a full-fleshed woman with all her curves in the right places. Her breasts pushed tightly against her red dress, which gleamed in the yellow light of the lamp. He could see the imprint of her nipples against the silk, and a smell of perfume floated from her body. Her gray eyes seemed to glow, as if with anticipation of excitement to come. His own body was already in a rage of hunger, and his britches were bristling with the shape of it. It was not a thing that would escape the practiced eye of a woman like her, and she smiled, aware of her power. Her breasts in front of him were irresistibly tempting, and he slipped his finger under her dress, eased out one breast, strikingly white, its nipple pink and erect with passion. He put his lips to it, flicked his tongue at the nipple, put his hand over her shapely butt. He stroked her body, lifted her dress, and unsurprisingly she wore only a silky chemise underneath, so that he touched the velvety skin of her butt. He brought his hand around to the front, stroked her soft mound, then parted the erotic crease, bringing his finger to the moist warmth within. He stroked her like this for a few minutes, and then, with a sigh, she kneeled, worked quickly to open his britches, brought out his ponderous potency, and with a quick movement took his fullness into her mouth. She moved deftly, deliberately, with intense hunger. She was daring in the movement of her lips and tongue, so that his pleasure sharpened, and the urgency of his desire made him withdraw abruptly. He quickly pulled down his jeans, while she, also caught by passion, flung her clothes aside. Her body was voluptuous, a high waist, full hips, shapely thighs and fleecy maidenhair over the erotic triangle. She slipped onto the bed, her rounded arms out, her thighs apart, looking on his bristling excitement. He put his body against the warmth of her flesh, caressed the silk of her skin, and she brought him to the lush warm opening. He slid deep into her, felt the marvelous soft flesh surround him and began to move. He kept firm control, and several times during his thrusting her body tightened, and she groaned as if her pleasure had pain in it. Then, feeling the rising surge, he began strong powerful thrusts that made her clench her teeth to keep from screeching, and then he felt himself swell to bigness and suddenly surge into her. It made her go wild and her body twisted this way and that, as if the feeling was too much to bear. They lay this way for a long time, coming down from a high way up.

After a while, they did it all over again.

The sun was almost down on the horizon and the sky all shot up with red and orange by the time he started back to the hotel. He walked on the red dirt street feeling nice and easy, the way he always felt after a good roll in the hay. Mady had been a smooth bit of silk and after roughing it on the trail, the right woman to bed down with.

A couple of wranglers rode by looking at him curiously, then a buggy loaded with provisions, driven by a boy sitting with an older woman. People were headed home to beat the coming dark. He glanced at the window of the general store, his mind on the supplies he'd pick up tomorrow morning, and was just passing the cowboy when the shot rang out. The cowboy yelped and dropped, Fargo

20

moved like lightning, crouched, his gun out, looking at two houses from where the shot might have come. Both were abandoned, two-story houses, and he stared hard, his gun ready for any sign of movement, but saw none. The cowboy was all right, just a flesh wound in his thigh, and was cursing softly.

"Are you all right?" Fargo asked, his eyes still searching for movement.

"Go get the bastard," the cowboy muttered, holding his thigh. Fargo raced to the side of the street and moved in a crouch toward the buildings. The shot, he was positive, was meant for him, and the cowboy an accidental victim. The same bushwhacker who had been trying to nail him from high ground on the trail—it had to be him.

He moved with quick light steps, hugging the side of the buildings until he reached the first house. He had to get this slippery character or one of his damned bullets might find its mark. His gun at the ready, he pressed tight against the walls, searched the top of the wooden steps, listened hard, heard nothing, no movement, no breathing. Moving light as a cat, he went up the steps, crashed into the empty room facing the street. Nothing. The wrong house! He went down in a rush to the doorway of the other house, repeated the same movements, but he knew from the beginning it was hopeless. The gunman had been elusive and clever up to now, managing somehow to shoot and run. It had become serious, the man had a hard grudge, whatever his goddamn reason, and was not giving up. On the second story, he found marks of the gunman all fouled; he covered his tracks. He had fired from here, one shot, made a run for it. Fargo's jaw clamped. He'd have to stay keyed up from now on, especially on the trail to Red Clay, where he was heading tomorrow. But this time *he'd* travel the high ground.

Fargo had just bitten into his jerky when he heard the bark of the gun and whistle of the bullet as it flew past his head. He went flat, crawled to the cover of a rock, his gun out. He swore softly, this time determined, once and for all, to nail this bushwhacker.

The hidden gunman always worked the high ground, clever strategy for it forced Fargo to scrabble up the slope, slowed him down, which was why the gunman got away. This time Fargo had taken the high ground.

I'll take this stinkin' hyena alive, he thought, and find out why he's been trying to blow my head off. He moved slowly on the crouch, from rock to rock, concentrating on a thicket of bushes, good camouflage for a smart gunman. As if to confirm his judgment, a bush quivered, and Fargo instantly put a bullet nearby to keep his man pinned down. This miserable critter had been sneaking shots for three days—he must have some crazy grievance. Well, he'd soon know. Fargo moved softly, quickly, his moves tricky, and it took almost twenty minutes to reach the thicket behind which he sensed a human presence.

His gun ready, every muscle alert, he moved an inch at a time, craning his neck for sight of his target. A few more silent movements brought his assailant into clear view. Fargo stood frozen, jolted: a young woman in Levi's, short black hat, tight checked shirt, red kerchief round her neck. She held a Colt, and dressed as she was, and seen from a distance, she could be easily mistaken for a cowboy.

Why in hell was she shooting at him? He'd never seen her before and couldn't imagine her grievance.

"Just don't move, miss, and you won't get hurt," he said, stepping forward. Her body stiffened, but she glanced behind at his gun, her jaw clenched, but she made no move. "Just open your hand slow and drop the gun," he said. When she did that, he crouched and tossed the gun into the brush, then crossed in front, scrutinizing her. An oval face, penetrating green-blue eyes, a small mouth with full lips, a long-waisted body, a fine chest and a bit leggy. What struck him was the hate and fear that shone in those green eyes, and he was convinced that given the slightest opportunity, she'd blast him to hell. He glanced at her horse tethered nearby; holstered rifle and saddlebag. The lady would pack a hefty punch, given the chance.

He sat on a rock facing her. "Why are you shooting at me, miss?"

Her lips tightened, but she said nothing.

"Do you know me?" he asked.

Her face stayed grim. "No, I don't know you."

"Why have you been shooting at me?" he tried again. She looked away, her green eyes smoldering.

"It was you who hit that cowboy this morning, in Eagle Butte."

Her eyes burned, but still she didn't speak.

"Aiming at me and hitting him. Not much of a shot, are you? You might at least be sorry."

"I am sorry," she said quickly, "that I missed you."

His face hardened. "You might tell me what you've got against me. Don't remember that our paths ever crossed."

Her mouth was a thin slit. "Oh they crossed all right."

"When?" he asked pleasantly. "I would remember you."

"We never met." Her voice was harsh. "But you met my family." She stared hard into his eyes. "My father, my brother, my mother. You met them. Four days ago." She watched him.

He scowled and thought back, and slowly a light dawned on him. He'd been riding the high ground toward Eagle Butte on his way to Red Clay when he saw a thin trail of smoke on an isolated crest of the hill. At the time he could use oats and water, and figured he might get some at the house. It took an hour to get there, and the smoke still curled out of the chimney. In the house he found a man, a woman and young boy, all dead. All had been shot, Fargo imagined, by passing drifters; the place looked looted and the man died with a gun in hand. It was a troubling scene and sent a rush of feelings over him as he remembered the wipeout of his own family. He felt a wave of compassion, and rather than leave the dead to prowling coyotes, he decided to bury them. This girl, he thought, apparently belonged to that family. But where had she been at the time of the shooting? Why'd she think he did it? It was damned strange.

The girl watched his face with a grim twist to her lips. She bent, as if to fix her shoe, scooped dirt and flung it at his eyes. Then she scampered toward her horse. It was an ancient trick and he shut his eyes before the dirt reached his face. He grabbed her halfway to her horse and she turned to claw at his eyes, but he kept her just out of reach; she kicked at his body, trying for his groin. A hellcat, surprisingly strong and out for blood. She probably figured that if he was the kind of man who'd kill her family, he wouldn't hesitate to include her in. In her mind, she was fighting for her life.

"Missy, I'm not going to hurt you," he muttered, trying to smother her swings and kicks. She kept kicking, aiming for his groin.

He finally got her arms together in a viselike grip so that she couldn't move, tumbled her down, he on top. She squirmed, twisted and hissed, like a captured snake struggling for escape, and he couldn't help but laugh. Her body was smothered under his and he could feel the warmth of her belly and breasts. It didn't take long for her strength to spend itself, and she lay still, breathing heavily, as if waiting for the worst.

He pulled her up, carried her to his pinto, uncoiled rope from his saddle, cut it, then tied her hands.

He sat on the rock, facing her. "Now let's have a talk. Why do you think *I* killed your family?"

There was a long pause while she studied him. Finally she spoke. "You buried them. To hide what you did."

"Why would I kill them?"

"You robbed them. Took our money."

He rubbed his chin. "So I took your money, did I? How do you know that?"

"I went into the house. I saw what was missing."

"How do you know *I* did the killing?"

She scowled. "Why else would you bury them? To hide your crime."

"You saw me bury them?"

"Yes."

"But you never saw me do the killing, just the burying."

She looked at him strangely. "I saw you when you were watching the stagecoach holdup."

He stared. "You saw that?"

"Yes, I was high on the crags above you. Waiting for you."

"I stopped hunting you," he said. "To stop the holdup."

Her eyes were narrowed. "Why didn't you shoot the Jones boys? Why'd you wait until the girl only was left?"

"You have a suspicious mind, missy. I was out of range."

Her eyes still glinted with disbelief. "But you could have fired. Might have saved lives."

"Well, little lady, I made a mistake. Didn't believe they would kill for money. They were crazy."

"But they were the Jones boys. Everyone knows they're killers. Where are you from?"

"Not from here." He paused. "I did shoot when I got into range. Now, let's get back to your family. You never saw me do the killing, just the burying."

She said nothing.

"Suppose I told you that I had come there to get some oats and water. That I found your family already dead?"

Her eyes narrowed and she looked away. Then looked back. "But why would you stop to bury them? It wasn't your business."

He nodded, and his teeth clenched as the anguish swept over him as he remembered the sight of his own family wiped violently out, just like hers. It took a full minute before he could answer, and she seemed startled by his expression.

"I'll tell you why," he replied, his voice sounding guttural. "I thought it was the whole family and didn't want the buzzards to get them. That was one reason. Second—it was that something like this happened to my own family. All of them, killed in cold blood, while I was somewhere else." He paused.

"Since then, my life has been mostly a search for those killers."

She was looking at him strangely, then suddenly her eyes filled with tears. She flipped to the ground and hid her face. He watched silently, aware that for the first time, probably, she let herself grieve for her family. That until now, rage and a lust for revenge had blocked her feelings of grief. He could understand, because fate had been merciless to them both in the same way. He pulled the knife from his shoe sheath and slit the ropes. She kept her face to the ground, still in the grip of her grief. He put his hand on her back to give comfort. She shivered and finally looked up, her face strained, her mouth twisted. Her green eyes glowed. "We are unlucky, the two of us," she said in a choked voice.

He felt a powerful urge to hold her close but he couldn't. Instead, he walked to the pinto and pulled out the coffeepot.

It was still a high sun, and the sky was pale blue with flimsy clouds. Two small purple flowers pushed out of the earth near the brush close by. A stray breeze carried a scent of pine.

They drank the warm fragrant coffee, and she soon seemed in better control.

"My name is Skye Fargo," he said.

She managed a smile. "Well, Mr. Fargo. I'm glad I'm a lousy shot. It might have been murder of an innocent man. My name is Julie Davis."

He grinned. "I'm glad you're a lousy shot too, Julie." He paused. "Have you any idea who did the killings? Someone with a grudge against your family?"

She shook her head. "No. No real enemies. We minded our own business. I had gone to Eagle Butte for a two-day visit with Mary Collins, a friend. I imagine, while I was away, a drifter probably came up to steal. He probably got Dad when he went for his gun. Then he killed everyone to hide the crime." Her lips tightened.

Fargo stroked his chin. "Three men did it. I looked at the tracks."

Her face hardened. "If only I knew who they were! If only I knew!" She clenched her fists.

Fargo sipped his coffee. He too felt vicious anger about the gunmen, and it was easy to feel her pain because it matched his own. He was unable to get a true fix on the killers of his own family, but in Julie's case, the trail was still hot and they could be tracked. Why shouldn't he help her? It would be, in a way, great satisfaction for him as well as for her.

"Miss Julie, do you want to pay those men back?" He watched her face.

"I'd give anything, anything."

He nodded. "I can help you find them."

Her face clouded with puzzlement. "But how? It's almost four days. We don't know where they are."

He emptied his cup of its coffee. "Well, Julie, I know something about tracking. We'll go back to your place, pick up their trail and follow them. And catch up with them, sooner or later."

Her eyes gleamed with hope. "Oh, God, if only we could!"

He stood up. "We can certainly try."

She too stood, took off her hat and shook her hair. It was golden blond, and reflected the gleams of the sun. He became sharply aware that she was really a beautiful young woman.

They rode back to her house and she went directly to the graves, stood silently over them. Fargo watched, his face stony, then spent the next half hour studying the prints. It didn't take long to reconstruct what happened. Three men, big and heavy, must have come at the house from the east, tethering their horses fifty yards away. They moved to the house on a crouch, one to the front window. The girl's father heard something because he went for his gun; he was shot from the window, which still had powder burns on its sill. Two men broke in the front door, cold-bloodedly shot the woman and the boy, then knocked things around until they found the money in a wooden jar hidden behind the bed. Then, cool and calm, they walked to their horses and rode east. To Fargo's practiced eye, the prints told the story as clearly as words. He studied the nicks and grooves in the hoofprints of the horses, fixed them permanently in his mind.

Julie had been watching his moves for the last five minutes.

"They've gone east," he said, and frowned. "Toward Waco."

"What is it?"

He scratched his chin. "Strange they should go back east. You'd think they'd go on west or somewhere else. Why go back?"

She shrugged. "They got plenty of money. That's what they wanted. Probably went back to familiar ground. To spend it there."

"How much did they get?"

She grimaced. "About one thousand dollars."

He was startled. "How'd your father happen to have that much? Not by farming at a place like this."

"Dad had always saved money. He came from east Texas where he had some good land with water. He sold it before he came out here. We could buy whatever we wanted, but Dad preferred to live quietly on this piece of land. He liked to mind his own business. We didn't like to mix around too much."

Fargo stroked his cheek thoughtfully. "So these drifters just stumbled on a good thing. With a thousand dollars they could go back to wherever they came from, gamble, guzzle and raise hell."

Her eyes were hard. "They had to be the scum of the earth to shoot down a woman and a boy."

He could feel what she felt, a cold, searing anger and an overpowering desire to confront these men. They'd become for him substitutes for the men who destroyed his own family, and who were for the time being still beyond his reach. These men, however, were not.

"How long would it take for us to catch up?" she asked.

He had been speculating on that himself. "It depends. They've got money. They'll stop and spend as they go along. That should slow them down. We'll catch up if we're lucky, in three days." He hitched his belt. "But we'll be traveling rough terrain. There are wild young Comanches between here and Waco. We might run afoul of them. The towns going east are still frontiers. We may have to eat off the land mostly. It won't be easy."

She glanced at the graves, and her eyes glittered with hate. "I won't rest easy until we catch up with them."

He too felt the burn of hate.

"Then let's start," he said.

It was easy enough to follow the trail, the three men apparently just cantering as if they were in no hurry, as if they had nothing to fear from behind.

They had done, Fargo thought, some sharpshooting: a bullet to the forehead of the father, two bullets to the heart for the mother and the boy. They were big men too; he could tell from the size of their occasional footprints. They had shot sharp and didn't seem to be afraid of much. You couldn't be careless with men like that.

Fargo and the girl rode silently through a meadow of yellow dandelions that stretched for a mile, then the land went smooth and hilly, then rocky and timbered. Now and then Fargo climbed upon rocks to survey distance or examine the ground. He soon picked up the prints of three other horses, prints he guessed were from Comanche ponies, Comanches, following on the trail of the men. Did it mean anything serious? Not really, for the men had to be days ahead. Still . . .

Then suddenly they saw ahead of them a thin swirl of smoke. Fire! The Comanches on a raid, he thought.

"What is it?" the girl asked, frowning.

"Comanches—I saw their prints."

Her lips tightened. "How many?"

"Three."

"It's an attack, isn't it!" she said.

" 'Fraid so. Probably an isolated cabin."

She bit her lip. "My heart goes out to them, Fargo, but we can't stop."

He stared at her hard. "We might be able to help."

Her jaw was hard. "There are already three killers running wild. That's our job."

He shook his head. "We've got to get into it." He put the pinto into a fast gallop, and after a moment, she followed him.

The smoke was thickening and he prodded the

31

pinto hard, swung up the hillside, through tall grass and thickets in an effort to approach the cabin from high ground. At fifty yards, he swung off the saddle, grabbed his rifle. "Stay here," he said to her. "I'll look. It may be too late."

He moved in a crouch, through grass and bushes. Then he heard the woman's scream, a terrifying thing, and it set his teeth on edge. A scalping! He moved as fast as he could. The Comanches would be busy plundering now, a good time to hit. He found a clearing between bushes. Smoke and flame were spiraling from the house. On the ground in front, a man was sprawled, his body riddled with arrows. He'd been scalped. And ten feet from him were two Comanches, their faces fierce with red paint, in breechclouts. They were standing over a woman spread-eagled on the ground. Her thighs and belly were exposed; she'd been raped. And scalped. One of the braves was holding up the scalp like a trophy. The woman's a goner, Fargo thought even as he had the scalper in his rifle sight. The bullet hit him right in the groin and flung him back staggering, limp as a ragdoll. He grabbed at his loins and screamed. Twice, Fargo thought, and shot at the groin again. Let the punishment fit the crime. The other Comanche started to race for rock shelter, but Fargo's next bullet slashed the side of his skull and he seemed to dive through the air and crash to the ground. Fargo's eyes swept the area. There was a third one; where was he? He'd seen three prints and there had to be one more. In the house, perhaps, looking for whiskey? The shots would have alerted him, but then, how long could he stay there? Smoke and fire must force him out. And whatever way he came, he'd be a target; Fargo waited. The smoke thickened, the flames danced and licked out of the window.

He wasn't there. Then where? A lone Comanche brave on the loose could do a hell of a lot of damage. Fargo began to move, alert to any movement. Nothing. He took a few precious moments to satisfy himself that nobody was near, then ran forward in a crouch. The woman was about twenty, pretty, her blue eyes open, shocked in death from the brutal scalping: she was better off dead. He turned to the Comanche lying nearby, the bloody scalp still clutched in one hand; he was still alive, still holding his groin, looking with hate-filled eyes at Fargo, who raised his rifle again. His bullet plunged through one of the Indian's eyes, splitting away the back of his head.

There was nothing more to do here. But what of the missing Comanche? An ugly thought hit him and he froze, then turned, started to race up the slope to where he'd left Julie. Gone! The tracks of two horses, an unshod pony and her sorrel. He cursed. Why hadn't he thought of the danger before! His pinto was grazing in a patch of tall grass. Fargo whistled sharply and the horse came running.

They could not be too far ahead and the Comanche had to be slowed down, Julie on her sorrel pulling behind him. Once he put his powerful pinto into a stretch he'd catch up. But he'd have to stay sharp, for the Comanche had her gun. He followed the tracks, and cursed when he realized the Comanche had shrewdly moved up onto the rocky hillside where he could find plenty of cover, where he could at any time stop and try for ambush. It meant Fargo would have to move slowly, carefully study every site for ambush. The trail went steeply up into a thickly wooded area, high-grown bushes and tall grass. Terrain like that, Fargo thought, had been chosen by the Indian for its camouflage, for concealment. He studied the lay of the land with care, then swung off the pinto and began his movements forward, first in a crouch, then as close to the ground as possible. Somewhere ahead, in that thicket of woods, bushes, boulders, Fargo's instinct told him, the brave would be waiting. Now it would be a pitting of skills, of trickery, and more than his own skin was on the line. He moved a few feet at a time, then stopped, listened, studied the shape of the landscape. He strained to hear: only the hum of insects, the sudden chipping of the redheaded woodpecker, then the smell of tart grass. Every cell in his body suddenly came alive: a copperhead snake, five feet away, raised its head, the beady black eyes staring directly at Fargo. He froze, scarcely breathed; the slightest sound would betray his position to the brave, waiting, he was sure, not more than thirty feet away. What would the snake do? If he started toward Fargo, he'd have to fire, and his position would be revealed. The snake's glittering black eyes seemed to plunge their gaze into Fargo's brain, it seemed so concentrated. Then, as if aware this human intended him no harm, it turned and slithered off to the right, its long black body twisting silently over the ground. Fargo realized then that he hadn't been breathing, and opened his mouth, gasping for air.

He crawled an inch at a time till he reached the decayed stump of a tree, and from there he peered at the ground in front of him. The brave was in there, he felt it, and he trusted his instinct: the brave would freeze, motionless, like a rock until the time came to strike. What, Fargo wondered, had he

34

done with Julie? Knocked her out? And if she came to, the Comanche would slit her throat in a moment to keep her quiet. So the first move was up to him. He needed a clue. There were three possible sites within fifteen yards, a twenty-foot boulder, a tangled mass of bushes and a crevice in the earth, where a man could easily hide. Beyond these sites, the ground was open and visible for thirty yards. The brave was in one of these three sites, hunched up, ready to strike. If Fargo could get just the whisper of a move, he'd be able to act. His eyes scanned the ground: a piece of rock big as his hand. Slowly, carefully, soundlessly, he reached for it. Now he had to make his decision, and he made it: the half-buried boulder, it seemed to him the most logical place for ambush, the most likely one, the one he'd choose for himself. He could be wrong, but he'd make a gamble—there was a problem of time.

He lofted the rock into a high trajectory to the right side of the boulder, and coming down it tipped the branches, rustled the leaves, a sound to startle and shock. Fargo moved in time with the sound, sprinting to the left side of the boulder, and there, big as life, was the Comanche, his red-painted face, his bronzed body in his breechclout, his gun aimed to the *right* at the sound. Half expecting him not to be there, Fargo was jolted at the sight, but it never stopped his move, for the brave, seeing nothing right, his head swiveled left, but before he could swing the gun, Fargo had fired, and a bloody hole appeared in his forehead as he hurtled back. He squirmed and went silent.

He found Julie squatted on the ground, her hands and feet tied, a rag stuffed in her mouth. She'd been dumped near the horses tethered to a tree almost fifty yards back. Her eyes were burning at him. He slashed the ropes.

She got up slowly, stamped her feet to circulate her blood, rubbed her wrists. Her blue-green eyes gleamed inscrutably.

Finally, she spoke. "What the hell took you so long, Fargo?"

He grinned; the lady had a lot of spirit.

Back on the trail, he picked up the tracks of the three men, and he and Julie rode on, a steady measured pace. They rode through a great cluster of cottonwoods, and the hooves of the horses crunched on some of the fallen leaves. When the sun started to slide, he made camp near a twisting rivulet. They pan-fried bread and meat, opened a can of beans. Julie, he thought, looked in good shape in spite of the rough handling by the Comanche.

"How'd that redskin get so close to you?" he asked.

"I'll never know. Never heard a sound. Suddenly he had my mouth covered, an iron grip. Then he hit me, knocked me out. When I woke, I was on the horse, my hands tied."

He chewed his meat. "But he didn't hurt you?"

"He had ideas, I could see. He didn't like what happened to his comrades. What'd you do to them?"

Fargo looked away a moment. "They raped and scalped the woman, killed the husband. I shot them."

She nodded. "Yes, I think my Comanche was thinking about revenge. A nightmare. Thanks for your help." She scowled. "Still, if you'd listened to me, we might have bypassed all that, it wouldn't have happened, we wouldn't be two hours behind schedule."

Fargo's voice was cool. "Maybe I didn't bypass that unlucky family for the same reason that I didn't bypass your family."

Her eyes clouded and she stared off into the distance. He lit a cheroot and his mind went back to the men they were tracking. Everything about them seemed so damned efficient; he'd seen their camping sites, picked cleverly, the way they fired their guns, the way they lucked into a lot of money. Were they just drifters or something else? They seemed to know what they were doing.

He warmed his hands on the coffee cup. "Where did you say it was your folks came from in east Texas, Julie?"

"I don't know exactly. He didn't talk about the past much. He often mentioned a place called Limestone. Why do you ask?"

He shrugged. "The way this trail is going, it wouldn't surprise me if we ended up in Waco. That's not far from Limestone. I just wonder if your dad ever had any trouble back there. This might be a feud."

Her eyes were somber. "He never talked about the past, I told you. Maybe it bothered him."

"What about your ma?"

"My ma is dead."

He stared at her.

"My real ma. She died when I was still a baby, my dad told me. That was my stepmother who got shot in the house."

He nodded. "And your own ma's dead. Seems like you lost your mother twice."

Her face was sorrowful. "Yes, twice." She stood up.

Fargo puffed at his cheroot. He sensed that there was more here than met the eye. Maybe they were not drifters after all. Well, he'd be extra careful, and sooner or later, he might find some answers.

The sky was dark blue and deepening. Fargo also

stood up, and stretched. He looked toward the grassy plain. A herd of elk was grazing there, watched over by a big-antlered stag. The stag, alerted by Fargo's movement, turned to stare hostilely; then, with dignity, he lowered his great antlered head and munched on the grass.

They had been riding east for two hours on high ground under the soft blue June sky spotted with cotton clouds when he heard the sound. He held up his hand and listened: a frantic drumbeat of hooves on the earth.

"What is it?" she asked.

"Two horses, running like hell for somewhere. Down there." He pointed to the trail that followed close to a small winding stream. Whatever it was, it looked like trouble. He swung off his saddle, pulled his rifle. It sounded like pursuit, two horses below the line of the cottonwoods; within minutes they'd be in the clearing.

"Take the horses back a bit. I want to look at this."

She frowned. "Let's not get into any business but our own, Fargo. We've got enough to worry about."

He nodded. "You don't know if you've got a friend or an enemy until you look."

She didn't like it, but took the reins of his pinto and trotted the horses back, tethered them to a branch. Then she came to where he had posted himself behind a fallen tree trunk.

They waited silently and it didn't take long for a white pony to come pounding out from behind the trees carrying a young woman, a Comanche. The speed of the pony sent the girl's black hair spinning behind her. She had a red headband, a short buckskin dress that revealed strong legs that kept pummeling the flanks of the pony. Her expression was definitely one of fear as she cast a quick look behind her. The reason soon emerged from the line of cottonwoods, a powerfully built Comanche on a black pony which he flailed unmercifully.

"What's going on?" whispered Julie.

He shook his head. Was it a lovers' quarrel or something much worse! The look on the girl's face suggested something more serious than a lovers' fracas. He watched grimly as the big black kept closing the gap and as the girl, in a desperate effort to escape, swerved sharply toward the stream. The Comanche, almost in a frenzy, closed in, grabbed the reins of her pony, bringing it to a snorting stop.

The girl jumped from the horse and started to run. The brave leaped after her, caught her by the hair and whirled her around. She suddenly stiffened, stared at him coldly, all resistance gone.

He shouted at her, his face distorted with fury. Her face stayed cold, impassive. He grabbed her two shoulders and shouted again. She said something, then he struck her, flung her to the ground. He was big-chested, with powerful arms. His bronze face was contorted. Whatever his grievance, Fargo thought, it was not going to express itself sexually. The brave pulled out his hunting knife, and its steel glittered in the sun. He looked down at her; she lay still, waiting courageously for death, her face calm. With a sudden decision, the brave dropped over her on his knees, raised the knife to plunge it into her heart.

"Fargo!" cried Julie.

But Fargo had already squeezed the trigger and the bullet struck the side of the Indian's skull, jerking him as if he'd been poleaxed, off the woman. His body twisted a moment, then stopped. The squaw, as if in horror, turned away, covering her face. Perhaps she expected another bullet for herself. Finally she turned to look at the dead man, then shut her eyes, as if her feelings were too much to handle.

Fargo, as he walked toward her, felt he'd done the right thing, though you never know—the squaw might have done something monstrous, but she didn't look the type. Nevertheless, a knife was not how you settled disagreements, he thought. She was standing now, looking to the high ground, and even from that distance, he was aware of her grace and dignity.

He came forward, Julie trailing. Closer, he could see her face, oval, sleek, like burnished bronze, the features put together perfectly, the mouth full-lipped and wide. Her hair was sleek and her eyes dark, glowing, and just now they were looking at him calmly.

"This brave was not your friend," he said ironically in dialect.

Her eyes glittered, as if with surprise that she could talk to him and convey her gratitude.

"Red Wolf my friend? He was my worst enemy. He wanted me dead."

"Easy to see. Why did Red Wolf want you dead?"

She looked off, as if the question brought pain. "Red Wolf was a great warrior. Wanted me for his woman. I would not be his woman. He told me then nobody else would have me. That it must be him or be my death."

Fargo couldn't help smiling. "What are you called?"

"Soft Cloud."

"I am Fargo. It seems to me, Soft Cloud, that it might be better to be alive and his squaw—than dead."

Her mouth twisted with feelings. "He was my enemy. He killed my brother, Little Eagle. I would die rather than betray the spirit of Little Eagle." Suddenly she turned to look back at the cottonwoods, her eyes shrewdly scanning the trees and land. He shot a glance there too.

"Does Soft Cloud expect more trouble?"

Her eyes looked at him calmly. "Red Wolf has brothers. They will come in time. They will know what has happened. I must go back to my own people."

Damn! That's all he needed. He glanced at Julie, who'd been listening to their interchange, not understanding a word. She seemed struck by the appearance of the girl. Now she spoke. "I didn't know you could talk to them. What's the pretty maiden saying?"

"She said the Comanche, Red Wolf, had wanted her for his squaw, but she hated him—he killed her brother. She turned him down. He's a great warrior and would not endure the insult. So she had to take him or take death."

Julie looked at her admiringly. "The lady has guts. Now what happens?"

He stroked his chin thoughtfully. "We give her escort, near her camp."

"Why can't she make it on her own?" Julie's eyes glittered. "They're very clever in the land, often better than we are."

He scratched his head. "There's a knot."

Her mouth hardened. "And that is?"

"It seems that Red Wolf has brothers. They're sure to come looking for him."

There was a long pause, then her voice went steely. "I told you, Fargo, that we should stick to our own business."

He shook his head. "You didn't like the idea, like me, of that Comanche putting his knife into that innocent Indian girl."

"No, I didn't. But it's not smart to hang around, to give her escort. It slows us down. We become a target. Haven't we got enough trouble?"

Fargo looked at the stream as it swirled and bubbled south. "We can't leave her alone." He thought of the cruelty of an avenging Comanche and didn't like the picture of Red Wolf's brothers paying off Soft Cloud for the killing that he had done. "We have to help her."

Julie didn't like it. "And what if we lose our three men?"

Fargo's jaw firmed. "We won't lose them."

Soft Cloud, he had noticed, had been watching them for a few moments, then she began to fix her hair. She straightened the broad red headband, folded her arms. Then she spoke. "Soft Cloud feels deeply about Fargo. He has given Soft Cloud her life. Now Soft Cloud must leave."

He was startled. "It is not wise for Soft Cloud to travel alone. The brothers of Red Wolf will come for revenge."

Her lids slid over the dark glowing eyes, as if she wished to mask her feelings. "The paleface squaw does not wish to go with Soft Cloud."

Fargo had to smile. Women could reach each other without language. "We must travel together. As three we are stronger than one. We will go with you until it is safe for you to reach your camp."

42

2

As they rode along, his remark—that three were stronger than one—came back to him, and he couldn't help but grimace. In truth, the women increased the risk. Three horses couldn't move softly; they clattered along the trail, it seemed to him, loud as a brass band. Sooner or later, he should expect an attack, and he searched the brush, trees, rocks, for telltale signs.

As they rode into a dense row of trees his nerves tightened. But off to the right, a herd of deer grazed peacefully, a good sign of man's absence. Just as this thought struck him, an alarm shot through the herd and they started to gallop.

Fargo, on the pinto, turned sharply to scan the area when the Comanche dropped behind him out of a tree, his knife glittering wickedly in his hand. But the whisper of sound, cloth on branch, had already mobilized Fargo's body. Even as he glimpsed the gleam of the sun on long steel, his arm shot up, halting the downward thrust, grabbing the thick wrist, holding it like a vise. He sensed another tree-dropping Comanche behind him in a scramble with Soft Cloud. Concentrating his strength, Fargo twisted the knife hand until he heard the wristbones break and saw the knife slip from limp fingers to the ground. He swung hard off the saddle, twisting

43

in midair, so that his body hit with a thud against the Comanche underneath—a rawhide, muscled body. He caught a glimpse of a fierce red face, and as they fell Fargo jolted his body hard against the Indian's, loosening his grip. Fargo turned slowly, pinned one hand, then with a powerful short punch to the jaw stunned his man just long enough to pull his gun, shoot at the Comanche who was carrying an unconscious Soft Cloud in his arms. He then saw Julie with a Comanche on top of her; she was struggling to get his hands off her throat, and instinctively, Fargo fired again. The bullet hit the Comanche's head, hurtling him off her body.

Under him, the Comanche moved suddenly, grabbing Fargo's gun hand with his undamaged left and straining every ounce of his strength to turn it toward Fargo. It took the most tremendous effort to halt that deadly movement. The Comanche, fighting for life, had the strength of the devil. The two men strained against each other, bodies and arms interlocked, muscles rippling. They seemed locked like that until Fargo felt a small give. Again they froze, then another slight give, and Fargo, moving a quarter inch at a time, suddenly squeezed the trigger. The body under him jumped; he fired again, this time at the chest. The Comanche quivered, and as Fargo pulled back he saw the black eyes, full of hate, suddenly go empty.

Julie was jarred by the attack, but she recovered fast; Soft Cloud took it stoically. He thought it smart to move out fast, and they rode south, toward Soft Cloud's people. Soft Cloud kept her pony to the rear, as if in care for the feelings of the paleface squaw. She had, Fargo felt, a nice sense of tact.

It was a hot, cloudless day and the sun glared

like a scorching eye. They kept to timbered land for camouflage. Still they rode sweaty in the heat, so that when they came to a cool, twisting stream, Julie insisted on bathing. Soft Cloud liked the idea, for she slipped off her buckskin and went stark nude for the water.

Julie was jolted and glared at Fargo, whose face registered admiration. Soft Cloud had a shapely bronzed body and strong thighs, dark hair between them. Fargo swallowed hard: the lust was on him—he was traveling with two beautiful women but could not make a pass, not yet at least. Not while they were dependent on him. He ground his teeth in frustration, then noted Julie scowling.

"Why don't you swim downriver, Fargo? The maiden doesn't seem to have much modesty."

"She doesn't have *false* modesty," he said. "A natural woman in a natural world."

"I don't mind a bit of false modesty," Julie said sardonically. "Downriver, please."

He grinned. "It's a pity we can't all be natural together."

"You can be natural—out of sight," she said.

He started to move down the stream, which twisted away from the women, when he was hit suddenly by the thought. It froze him in his tracks. He'd been nagged by the thought ever since the Comanche attack. His skin tingled, he shook his head, then nonchalantly followed the curve of the stream, glancing back as if to check the sky. But his gaze raked the ground, the gulleys, the trees, the rocks. Wherever the Comanche could hide. Because there had to be one more Comanche out there—that was the thought that nagged at him.

Just before the Indian attack, he remembered, the deer herd started to run. Why? Why just then?

There had to be a Comanche to start that run—diversion at the right moment. This Comanche had been too far to get into the fight, but he'd not give up—vengeance for the death of a brother burned hot in the Comanche heart.

Fargo would bet his bottom dollar that out there a Comanche was waiting to strike at the right moment.

Such as now, when the tall paleface would swim and leave his gun on land in his Levi's. Fargo lit a cheroot to give himself time to scan again the terrain. Nothing. Not yet, but he had to be there. A clever Comanche who knew he'd have to hit the big paleface to get Soft Cloud.

How to lure this redskin out, Fargo wondered? Get into the stream but hug the land, so that, at first sight of the enemy, he could race for his gun? He could be caught bare-assed. He ground his teeth—it was a stopper.

But what if there was no one out there after all! What if he was just working up a lot of bad pictures in his head? No, that Comanche had to exist or the deer herd never would have started; it was triggered at a prearranged time when, on the trail, he passed under the trees. Maybe the Comanche had gone back to his tribe for reinforcement? Why had he not attacked before this? Not easy to get close, the way they traveled.

He moved to the edge of the stream, turned so he could see behind him; he took off his shirt, started to pull off a boot. Then he paused as if in thought.

There! A movement, just the ghost of a movement, and it could be human. In a small crevice, seventy yards back, and in it lay either a lurking Comanche or an animal. He scratched his head, pretended to change his mind about a swim, put his shirt on and

46

started forward, managing always to stay behind a tree, a rock, always some cover.

When he reached the women, Julie let out an indignant yell. He couldn't help glancing at her: the water was just below her hip line and he could see her shapely breasts, the nipples, the slender waist, the fine spread of hips and the patch of golden hair. She dropped into the water, yelled again at him, but he had already turned and was moving toward the crevice, his gun ready. There was a line of bushes, trees, just beyond the crevice, which made it a fine hiding place. He moved zigzag until he could see into the crevice. Empty! But the signs were clear—moccasin prints, prints of a body. He'd been there, the Comanche, and moved like lightning the moment Julie yelled, diverting Fargo. Now he was into the tree thicket and it'd be rough going after him, especially in the darkening light. Two things were clear: the Comanche had no gun or he would have used it. And he was going to stick to them until he got close enough to use his tomahawk or knife.

From now on, when they rode, he'd have to keep that Comanche in mind. If Fargo knew one thing, it was that the Comanche could be the most dangerous opponent—he could blend into the land, lie still as a log, seem part of a tree, come out of the ground. Fargo told himself he'd have to concentrate; to be a second late could be fatal. And concentrating wouldn't be easy traveling with two women. Already he could sense the tension between them. Soft Cloud remained wrapped in cool dignity and Julie, when she looked at the Indian girl, couldn't keep the glint of hostility out of her eyes. She blames Soft Cloud, he thought. She's burning for revenge, she wants to go for the killers of her family and Soft Cloud is an interference. He shrugged. But that was life: you take one trail; Fate plays a joke and you find yourself on another. What the hell—she didn't have to throw a fit: with patience and good headwork they'd be back on the trail again. Soon they would drop Soft Cloud and pick up the hunt. And while he felt vicious, because in his mind the hunted men stood for the killers of his own family, still he couldn't let Soft Cloud pay for his killing of Red Wolf.

They rode south and he took the wide, grassy land, which would force the Comanche to stay back or move north and skulk through timbered country.

At sundown they camped in a grove, sheltered with trees; he must stay alert. By midnoon tomorrow, he figured, they would leave Soft Cloud safe with her people and again pick up the trail of the killers.

After eating, they sat around the fire sipping coffee. Julie stared at him, frowning. "I didn't know, Fargo, that you are a Peeping Tom. It surprised me; you didn't seem to be the type."

He scowled. "What?"

"You were supposed to be swimming, out of sight, downstream. Instead you double back and there you are, catching us in our skins."

He looked past her at the darkening sky; it'd be night shortly, a time when things could happen. "You may be surprised to hear this. But I didn't come to stare at your body. Very beautiful, by the way, but to make sure we didn't have an uninvited visitor—while we were swimming and easy to pick off."

Her green-blue eyes clouded. "What do you mean? There were three Comanches."

He sighed. "There's a *fourth*. The one who stampeded the deer."

She stared. "Has he been trailing us?"

He nodded. "I found his prints. He was waiting for me to get into the water. He's a sly one, moves like a damned shadow. Maybe the most dangerous of them."

"Damn!" That's all she said, but stared with hard eyes at Soft Cloud. Fargo sipped his coffee. She was blaming the girl for their danger and blaming him for getting trapped by the girl.

"We should have stuck with our own business, Fargo," she had told him. And now, he thought, she was worried about a crafty Comanche creeping in during the night. And just because he couldn't put the two women at risk, to pursue the Comanche, the Indian could choose his time and place of attack. Fargo glanced about the grove, searching always for hint of movement.

Then Soft Cloud spoke. "The paleface squaw is unhappy that I am here, Fargo. Tell her I will be gone when the sun is high again." Her features, he couldn't help but think, were lovely, the straight nose, the charming oval face, the big glowing black eyes that could not conceal the warmth of the woman.

"How did Red Wolf come to kill Little Eagle?" he asked, pouring more coffee from the pot into his cup.

Her face registered pain at the thought of her brother. She spoke slowly. "Red Wolf wanted me for his squaw and came to court, but I did not like his ways. He had the ways of the wolf, cunning, hungry, unjust. His anger was great and his pride hurt because I did not welcome his attention. To hurt me he began to mock Little Eagle, mocked his

49

manhood. And my brother felt forced to fight. A knife fight. And Little Eagle had only seventeen summers." She paused and her eyes went moist.

Her words made him grimace: it was nice to shoot a man like Red Wolf and find out later he was a rotten skunk. "It was a good time for Red Wolf to die," he said.

She smiled, then looked at the land. "It is wise for Fargo to be watchful. The brother of Red Wolf moves about us like the mountain lion that wishes to rip and to kill."

So, she too knew the Comanche was skulking about in the brush, waiting for the right time to strike.

He smiled. "Fargo will be sad when Soft Cloud has gone."

Small fires seemed to burn in the depths of those dark eyes. "It is twice now that Fargo has saved the life of Soft Cloud. Much is owed to Fargo."

He smiled again. The Comanche that he'd shot was carrying Soft Cloud off—off to what? Probably to a degrading experience. It was how the braves would make her pay for what happened to Red Wolf. They'd pleasure themselves, maybe destroy her, even though it was Fargo's bullet that killed him. Comanche logic. Her lovely, bronzed face gleamed in the firelight and it was easy to read her warm feelings.

"What the devil is she talking about?" demanded Julie suddenly. "Is she making a love offer to you?"

Fargo grinned. "You wouldn't be a touch jealous, would you?"

Julie's voice hardened. "Fargo, let's be clear about one thing. We're together to destroy three rotten dogs. That's the only idea I have in mind. I don't think beyond that." She paused and glared. "But if you're starting to moon like a lovesick calf with this Indian maid, you'll lose your concentration. I need a man with iron in him to help me kill three killers. Not a cowboy who loses his head when a pretty Indian maiden flutters her eyes at him."

Fargo rubbed his cheek. This filly had a tongue like the sting of a wasp. Yet he had to respect her single-minded obsession. It didn't matter whether she was jealous or not, all she wanted was revenge for her family, and everything that blocked that was hateful to her. Especially this beautiful Indian girl, who not only pulled them off the trail, but now entangled Fargo in her feelings. No, it wasn't jealousy that made Julie talk waspish; it was her lust for revenge.

"Don't worry your pretty head. By tomorrow noon, we'll be after our men again. I want them as bad as you. And whatever else happens, nothing will stop us."

She shrugged, but the skepticism in her eyes was clear as crystal. Well, he wouldn't bother his head about it.

He lay on the bedroll, his hands clasped behind his head, and looked at the night sky. The sickle moon cast a dim light on the earth; the shadows of boulders and trees were heavy—a good night for a Comanche to camouflage movement. What did he look like, Fargo wondered? A brother to Red Wolf would be powerfully built, with a muscular chest. And the Comanche would know that Soft Cloud was only half a day away from her people.

The Comanche, he felt sure, would try and close in on this night, perhaps his last chance; Fargo had his gun inches from his hand. Before he had settled for the night, he examined the ground nearby, looking at every ambush site. He had them mapped in his mind. His eyes felt heavy, and he knew, before long, he'd dive into sleep. The image of Julie standing in water to her hips came back, and he couldn't help but grin, remembering her astonished look, which switched to indignation at the sight of him. The look of her body hit his mind vividly, the sensual hips, slender waist, full breasts and golden hair between her thighs. He felt steamy; he was horny as a goat. And, damn, there was a long stretch before he'd find a woman. He ground his teeth, frustrated, shut his eyes, and after twisting restlessly, slipped into sleep.

He heard the sound, he always heard sound in sleep, because part of his mind on the trail stayed alert, a big reason he managed to keep alive. The sound was soft; it made him think Indian, but lightweight Indian. His fingers were inches from his gun, but he felt no need to reach. The Indian was Soft Cloud, and she came slowly, as if waiting for him to open his eyes. She was ten feet away, crawling on her stomach toward him. She knew he was awake, then continued to crawl. Fifty feet behind a tree trunk, Julie slept on her bedroll, dead to the world.

He wondered if Soft Cloud had heard the Comanche and come to warn him. Her black eyes gleamed in the pale moon, and the top of her breasts showed under the loose buckskin dress. She stopped at his side.

"Soft Cloud has heard the brother of Red Wolf?" His voice was low.

"He is somewhere near—now—waiting and watching." Her face was composed, unafraid, but her nostrils flared to show her feelings.

Fargo listened, heard nothing, put his finger to his lips, whispered, "Stay." And turned for his gun. Suddenly his nerves screamed and he wheeled just in time to see the frenzied eyes of the Comanche with raised knife. Fargo's arm went up instinctively, caught the thick wrist, stopping the downward thrust of the cruel-looking knife. The Comanche twisted wildly to break Fargo's hold. He could glimpse the powerful bronze body, thick features, high cheeks. The knife, just three inches from Fargo's neck, if it moved, could split him like a melon. Fargo held on, bringing all the power of his back muscles, forcing the Comanche's arm to turn until the tendons in it began to tear, the fingers open and the knife drop. Fargo shoved the Comanche, making him stumble, grabbed the knife, and lightning fast plunged it into the Comanche's back, twice. The Indian groaned, twisted, went slowly still and silent.

Fargo took two deep breaths, then grabbed the Comanche's body and pulled it into the bushes at least a hundred feet from the scene of the fight.

When he came back, Soft Cloud was where he'd told her to stay. And nearby Julie was standing, her eyes glittering, her gun in hand.

She shook her head. "I couldn't get a shot at him, Fargo. Might have hit you. But he'd never come out of it alive."

He managed a smile. "Glad you were there. Well, I guess we can sleep easy for the rest of the night. We need the rest."

"You're all right, Fargo?" Julie asked, a bit anxious.

"Not a scratch," he said.

She glanced at Soft Cloud again, a glitter in her eyes, as if to let her know she was the cause of this gruesome night fight.

Fargo had to smile.

Quiet settled over the night, but it seemed only minutes had passed before he heard her crawling back. Soft Cloud made sure he was awake. "Soft Cloud has brought much trouble to Fargo," she said.

He smiled. "It is not trouble to Fargo. Tomorrow you'll be safe with your people."

"Yes, tomorrow Soft Cloud will leave Fargo forever. It's very sad. Fargo too has said he is saddened."

He felt his skin crawling as he tried to make sense of her words.

"Soft Cloud has come to say good-bye to Fargo," she said, then stood up, pulled at the shoulder of her buckskin dress and it fell, revealing her body. The bronze of her deep breasts glinted in the moonlight. He could see her splendid thighs, the dark pubis, the finely molded body. Fargo's own body, which had been seething for a woman, came alive. Offered a prize like this, he didn't pause a moment to discuss the wherefores but reached for her. He brought her body next to his; her flesh was silken and firm, and he buried his face between her breasts, then kissed the nipples, touched his tongue to one. His body felt inflamed and he fondled her breasts for a time, then his hand went down between her thighs, caressing the mound, then slipping into the velvet warmth. He kept stroking while fondling her breasts, then her hand reached for his pulsating hardness. She caressed it gently, then dropped to her knees, rubbing it against her breasts, her cheeks, kissing it over and over. He eased her to the bedroll, slipped over her body, feeling its luxurious firmness, felt her thighs widen, and he slowly slipped into the lush warmth. She was tight and he felt a fierce desire to thrust hard, but held off, moving slowly at first, his hands grasping her silky buttocks. Her firm body rose to meet his movements, which began to quicken. Each stroke brought him sharp pleasure and he found the firmness of her flesh marvelous. His hands under her smooth buttocks lifted her to his movement, which became more vigorous; they went on and on until he was thrusting into her violently. He could hear her gasps, her small moans, and then, as his tension reached its pitch, he plunged frantically and felt himself go rigid, then explode. Her body twisted as if she was in torture. She kept twisting and he could feel her heart beating frantically against his chest.

He lifted his body, still in the throes of pleasure, and there came from her a moment of strange total silence, a concentration that seemed to have nothing to do with love—then she cried "Fargo!" And her body came up in front of him, protectively, even as he dimly saw the shape, heard the twang of the bow as the arrow buried itself in her back. His hand moved like lightning, as if it had its own mind, and his gun fired. The guttural cry told him he'd hit the target and the dim shape fell crashing in the bushes.

That damned Comanche had not been dead, had crawled to get his bow and arrow, and somehow, on sheer guts, returned to kill.

He looked at Soft Cloud. Her face was twisted in pain, and her eyes were on him—then her face became composed, serene even, and she smiled as she closed her eyes in death.

Julie, at the sound of gunfire, had crawled toward him, gun in hand. When she saw Soft Cloud, she stared a long moment. Fargo pointed in the direction of the Comanche, and Julie turned and crawled toward him. She found him in the bushes, his red muscled body still looking powerful though he sat there dying. As she came toward him, with agonized effort, he reached for an arrow to put into his bow. His movements were slow but determined. She watched him a moment, then she fired, hitting his chest.

He went down in slow motion, striking the ground with his head first. He closed his eyes and died.

Fargo buried Soft Cloud under a big beautiful oak with wide sweeping branches. The tree had to be as big as her spirit. Soft Cloud had put her body between him and the arrow meant for his death, her last act before she'd given him love. How do you pay a debt like that? He had cradled her in his arms a long time before he put her down.

Then he dropped her into the grave and stood over it. The sky was pink, and Julie sat on a nearby boulder, looking at a mountain peak, far off, that reached for the sky.

3

After he buried Soft Cloud he stood over her grave, silent, head bowed, while Julie watched. Her face was grim and her gaze restless as if she expected another Comanche to slip out of the bushes and again block her from the one thing she wanted above all others—revenge. But the woods were quiet. She looked tense, in a rage to ride, but dared not show it. Finally Fargo turned from the grave and moved to the horses.

By the time they picked up the trail, the sun was high in a radiant blue sky; they rode hard to try and make up for lost time. Julie said little, aware that he'd been hit by the way Soft Cloud died, protecting his body with hers.

They rode most of the time in silence and finally reached Little Creek, a rough town with the usual saloon, hotel, cowboys and drifters. He thought of the men they were hunting. "They stopped in the saloon, you can bet on it, for drinks, cards, women."

"I'll go with you," she said.

He smiled, thinking the men in the saloon would get the wrong idea. "Why not clean up at the hotel. I won't be long."

"Well, I could stand a bath and a good warm meal. But let me know what's happening. I want to be there, if something starts."

He nodded. She gazed at him steadily. "I hope you're not going to drink hard. I know you have an excuse for it. But there's a job to be done. We can't waste time."

His lips barely twisted. "I don't drink hard, and I never waste time. But I'd do it if I wanted to."

Her lips tightened, and she booted her horse. He watched her move to the hotel, then stopped at Riley's Saloon, tied the pinto to the rail post. As he reached the swinging door he tensed and his hand leaped to his Colt at the sound of gunshot. A groan told him someone had been hit. He waited, then opened the door carefully. A dead cowboy on the floor, shot in the chest. At the far end of the bar a lean, tall grim-faced man, dark-haired, with a red kerchief, was slipping his gun into its holster. Men who had been standing against the side walls came forward; obviously the fight was over.

"Let's clear the floor," said the barman, who had to be Riley, a bald, stout man in an apron. Two men took the dead cowboy through a door in the back. The drinkers gathered at the bar and talked in low tones, and a card game that had been interrupted by the gunfight started again. The big, lean man threw a glance at Fargo, then returned to his chair in the card game, where the quarrel seemed to have started.

Riley, the barman, looked at Fargo. "A little disagreement," he said, and shrugged, as if killing because you disagreed with someone was not an idea he could ever understand. "What'll it be?"

"Whiskey."

Riley slapped a shot glass on the scarred wooden counter, filled it and left the bottle. His gray, washed-out eyes ran over Fargo, the grime of travel.

"Just hit town?"

Fargo nodded and lifted his glass.

"Where yuh headed?"

"East." The men at the bar, Fargo noted, were listening. In towns like this everyone wanted a fix on strangers. It was natural curiosity and a chance to hear some news. "How's the territory?"

"The Comanches are out there," Riley said, grinning. "Wouldn't surprise me if you had to run through them."

Fargo grunted and lifted his drink.

"Did you, mister?" Riley persisted.

"The name's Fargo. They're back there, all right. Ripped into a home five miles west, on a hill."

The bar became silent, listening.

Riley looked troubled. "That'd be Bill and Maisie Gilbert. What happened?"

Fargo poured another shot from the bottle. "It was bad. Both of them gone. Scalped. Comanches. Three. Tried to burn the house." He sipped his drink.

There was a long pause. "Three?" Riley said. "Did you see them or see their tracks, Fargo?"

Fargo twisted the glass in his fingers. "Saw them."

A heavy silence. Nobody was drinking, even the cardplayers had stopped playing.

Then the big lean man who'd shot the cowboy spoke from the table. "Can one ask, mister, what happened when you saw them?" He had yellow eyes, a tough leather skin and his voice was toneless. There seemed to be a silent threat about him.

Fargo didn't like the look of the man, but he smiled. "I did what any red-blooded man would do. Shot them."

"All three?" asked Riley.

"All three."

Riley filled his glass. "Have one on the house, Fargo."

The bar came alive with the murmur of voices. A white-headed old-timer at the end of the bar gulped his beer, wiped his mouth. "It's a pity about Maisie. Going to have a baby too."

"I told Bill," said a cowboy, "to come into town till things quieted down."

"Well, Fargo paid them off," said Riley. "They're picking off the outpost houses. Wonder if they're putting out war parties."

"Naw," said the old-timer. "Just some wild young braves who want whiskey, horses and to kick up their heels."

Fargo leaned toward Riley and spoke in a low voice. "I'm interested in three men, big men, who may have stopped off here about three days ago. Happen to see them?"

Riley's eyes skidded to the table. "That's one of them, right there. Bowie. Had a falling out with Joadie and Red. Bowie just stayed behind. Fast with a gun—as you just saw."

Fargo hitched his jeans. From the beginning, he had a feeling about Bowie; he was big, tough and ready with his gun. Better move slowly. Bowie was sitting at the card table with three players, and looked deep in the game. You didn't break up a game like that. It would be better to get him later, corner him somewhere and squeeze the story out about that killing. There had to be one. Why should three men come west, stop at one house, knock off the people, lift more than a thousand dollars. They must have known something. Since he could do nothing just now, he'd go over to the hotel and tell Julie he was on to something. Perhaps, by that time, Bowie would be out of the game.

He nodded to Riley, who watched him leave with a curious smile. At the hotel, he found Julie in the dining room, a plate of fried chicken, black-eyed peas, okra. Her lovely face glowed with health and she smiled blissfully. "Nothing like it, Fargo, a bath and hot food." He took the chair at her table and signaled to the waiter. "Bring me some of that."

"So, Fargo, I'm glad to see you're not drunk."

He scowled. "I drink as I please, as I do everything else."

She smiled. "I'm feeling good right now, don't spoil it."

He shook his head; she was a ripper. "I think that one of our men is at the saloon."

She stared at him and her face hardened. "Are you sure? How do you know? Where are the others?"

"I'll make sure. We should move slow. He's one of three men who came to town three days ago. Bowie, that's his name. He had a disagreement with the two others, named Joadie and Red. They left without him."

She stood. "Let's get him."

"Hold your horses. We should move slow, I said. He just had a bar fight, killed a cowboy. Now he's in a card game. I'll go back after I eat. I want him out of the game. I want to corner him, talk to him." He rubbed his chin. "After I leave here, give me ten minutes, then walk toward the saloon. Maybe things will start to clear up."

"I don't like that," she said, her face grim. "I want to be there."

He shrugged. "Do it my way."

She watched him eat, her eyes glowering, and when he moved out of the dining room later, anger was still on her face.

He walked down Main Street—it was red dirt

with badly built white clapboard houses on each side—and approached the saloon. He was startled to see Bowie, slouched against the rail post, his hat low over his eyes, waiting, and it was clear for whom. About five men, he recognized from the bar, were standing on the porch, also watching. Showdown, Fargo thought: he'd seen men like this before, tense, quiet, the way men were when they expected to see a killing. Fargo walked easy, though his body was mobilized for action. That damned Riley was a blabbermouth, that's why Bowie was waiting. The sun burned hard and he pushed his Stetson back, keeping his eyes on Bowie. When he got about ten feet in front of the tough, leather-faced man, he spoke. "Hold it right there, mister." Fargo stopped, stared into the yellow-brown eyes that were glittering dangerously.

"I hear you were asking about me. About me and my friends. That right?"

The sonofabitch was cocky as a pixilated rooster; he had a lot of confidence, thought himself the hottest gun in the territory; well, maybe he was.

"Yes. I was asking about you."

"Well, Fargo, ask straight out. What d'ye want to know?"

Fargo's eyes were icy. "I want to know if you and your two friends stopped at a house near Eagle Butte and did some killing."

Bowie's face tightened with sudden anger. He didn't like the sound of that, especially in front of his saloon friends. "You got it wrong, Fargo. We rode up, wanting some directions. The lousy coyote in there started shooting at us. So we went in."

There was a long pause.

"So you went in and killed the woman and a boy of fourteen."

Bowie flushed. "They were using guns too."

Fargo smiled grimly. "And then you kicked everything around and took a thousand dollars from under the bed."

Bowie stared, his eyes in wide shock. "Who told you that crazy story, mister?"

"For one thing, Bowie, I was there. And I didn't see any guns on that kid or woman. And the man never fired a damned bullet. His gun wasn't even cocked. And I heard there was a thousand dollars in ready cash, in the house."

Bowie ground his teeth, slipped a glance at the men on the porch—their faces were grim—he'd lost them. He studied Fargo. This man had balls to make an accusation like that—either he was a blasted fool or a hot gun. The trouble was he didn't have time to find out which—he'd promised the men at the saloon a piece of entertainment, but it had turned out sour. He had to make his move.

"Are you calling me names, Fargo?"

Fargo's smile was icy. "A liar, a coward, a thief and a lowdown killer of women and kids."

Nothing on the street moved for a moment, then Bowie went for his gun. He was fast, everyone said so, and he got it out of the holster, but Fargo's bullet by that time had hit his chest. Bowie staggered back three steps, then collapsed like a bag of sawdust.

Fargo, looking at the body, felt a twinge of regret. He'd been stupid. Bowie was dead, and whatever he knew about Julie's family was dead too. But what could he have done—Bowie, alerted by the barman, had forced the play. From the corner of his eye he could see Julie practically on the run from the hotel. She'd heard the shot and came up fast to where he was standing near the body.

She flashed Fargo a strange look, then stared hard at Bowie lying there, his yellow eyes wide open, as if in shock that he'd lost the gunfight. After long moments of looking, she spoke, her eyes still on the dead man. "Was he one of them, Fargo?" Her voice was cold.

"Bowie, that was his name. He was one." She kept looking at the body as if she couldn't get enough. "Well, there's two more." But the look she gave Fargo was hard as the one she gave to Bowie.

They rode east toward Pottsville and the prints of their quarry were unmistakable. Julie scarcely spoke; she was hard-faced and brooding. The trail went through timbered country, flat country, rocky country, and Fargo scanned the land with a keen eye. Back in Little Creek, the old-timer had judged the Comanche raid to be that of wild young braves, not the work of a war party, and Fargo was inclined to agree. There wasn't hide or hair of a Comanche, and the landscape simmered peacefully in the hard sun. It was a sweltering day and the flanks of the horses became wet with sweat. They pitched camp about five miles west of Pottsville to let the horses feed in the shade. The sky looked like a blistered tin sheet to Fargo, and around them great rocks shot up from the earth, some shaped like dominoes.

The brooding look on Julie's face stayed, but he said nothing, thinking that sooner or later, she'd make her squawk.

It came finally when they were drinking coffee. "Fargo, I'm grateful, of course, that you took care of Bowie, but that was not all that I wanted." Her green-blue eyes caught the light of the sun and seemed burning with resentment.

"What's that mean?" He almost scowled at her.

"It means you shut me out of what happened. Put me on the shelf in the hotel. I don't want to see *just a dead body*. That's not enough." Her lovely face twisted with feeling. "These men killed my family in cold blood. My father, mother and little Bill. They suffered, they went through hell." She stopped to clear her throat, choked up with feelings. "That's what I want to see. A dead body is something, but it's not enough." Her voice hardened. "When you told me you had spotted Bowie, I wanted to join you. I asked you, but you shut me out."

He frowned. "You don't understand. Women like you don't go into these saloons."

Her eyes glittered. "I'll be the judge of where I can go—not you. I want to be there. I want to see these men, and if I can, want to do the killing."

He lifted his coffee cup. She was a rip-snorter of a woman. She had poison in her blood and wanted to get it out. He remembered back in Eagle Butte, when she was shooting at him, he thought her a wild young buck, and she'd almost punctured him. But she wore Levi's, and filled them with a full, rounded womanly body. Still, he could understand her feelings. He thought of how she had stared at Bowie's body, as if it just wasn't enough to see him dead. She wanted to see what *he* had seen; Bowie's fear, his squirming, his guilt and his dying. When he had killed Bowie, wasn't he, in a strange way, taking revenge on the killers of his own family? But that's what *she* wanted—all the sweetness of revenge!

"All right," he said. "From now on, you come along. Even to the saloons. That's what you want, right?"

Her face softened, and with it all her femininity

65

came back. "That's what I want, Fargo. Now—there's two to go. Where do we find them?"

"Don't know exactly. They went toward Pottsville. We'll find out something there. The saloon, of course."

She reflected. "All right. I don't have to go to the saloon right off. But I want to be there—if there's going to be action."

He smiled. A saloon could turn from a peaceful drinking place into a gunfighting hell in the space of minutes. Whiskey, lots of it, turned quiet men into roaring lions and they'd pull their guns at the wrong word, wrong smile. And a green-eyed looker like Julie walking into that setting could start fireworks too. Not always, but just in case, he'd be there.

4

There were towns in Texas, Fargo knew, that pulled the wild men of the territory like a magnet. Pottsville was one of these towns. As he and Julie walked their horses down Main Street past houses that were crude and unpainted, he looked into the faces of men. Drifters with hollow eyes who'd probably shoot a man for the belt on his Levi's. They seemed to be the backwash of the territory, men wanted elsewhere by the law: con men, cutthroats and killers. And the women there seemed to cater to the needs of such men. And a sprinkling of solid citizens who made the town work.

They were riding to the Lone Star Hotel and had almost reached the front of the saloon when the doors swung open and two big men came out. They were flushed from drinking and one, with ferret features, stared bold-eyed at Julie.

"Hey, Ray, look at the tits on that filly." His voice was harsh and loud.

Ray had been looking and he drawled, "Lotta good times in a filly like that, Johnny boy."

"That's one lucky cowboy," said Johnny.

"Is that right, cowboy," said Ray insolently. "Must be a lotta fun in a filly like that." And he caught the pinto's reins and grinned wolfishly.

"Whaddya say, cowboy, would you lend us the filly for the day?"

Johnny laughed hysterically. "Yeah, sorta rent her out. We'll keep her busy, so she won't be lonely for you."

"Yeah," said Ray, "Johnny's got a *big* idea on how to do it."

Both laughed uproariously, at each remark, as if they were the wittiest in the world.

Fargo couldn't believe his ears. They had to be stark, staring crazy drunk to pass such cracks. Wherever Fargo moved in the territory, even among those who didn't know his name or his speed with a gun, he managed to draw respect, or at least caution. He was tall, powerful, sinewy and moved like a mountain cat, and something in his face made men think twice before they made a move against him. Unless, of course, they were deep-down stupid or vicious. And these men easily qualified for both. He would have jumped from his horse long ago to cut their comedy if it hadn't been for Julie and that he was committed to her mission.

"Pay no attention," said Julie softly. "They're drunk and not what we're after."

Fargo gritted his teeth. "Let go the reins, mister."

Ray stared at him insolently. "What, what. You're not gonna take that filly away from us, cowboy. We can't let that happen, can we, Johnny? Tell yuh what. You stay here, and Johnny and I will take good care of your filly." So saying, he jerked at Fargo. It was so unexpected that Fargo fell clumsily to the street.

This set off a burst of laughter from a string of loafers on the porch and railing, men always on the search for amusement, and they sensed it coming. But when the big, lean stranger got up and looked at them, his lake-blue eyes like points of fire, they stopped laughing.

Julie too looked at him and her voice pleaded. "Fargo."

His voice was harsh. "Don't interfere."

He turned to Johnny and Ray, who had slapped their knees, amused at his clumsy fall. They were bulky men, stubble-bearded, in scruffy Levi's and flat black hats. They wore Colts with smooth handles. They sensed something in Fargo and moved near each other. But their faces were insolent and smirking. They had no fear, Fargo thought, because they were two and didn't dream he'd make a move against two guns—typical bully thinking.

"I don't hear too good," he said to Johnny. "But I think you were trying to make a remark about the lady."

Johnny's dark eyes studied him without a spark of intelligence—they had only the gleam of an animal's cunning.

"I just said the lady's a fine filly. And that if you need help to keep her happy . . ." He grinned at Ray.

"We'd be glad to oblige," finished Ray, and he grinned back. "Whaddya think?"

Fargo looked at their faces, could see only cruelty and wolfish cunning. They were scum who'd done their share of killing somewhere else and ended up safe in this stinkhole. And in a place like this, they thought they could do what they wanted and get away with it. All for fun. And they'd put on a show for the hangers-on nearby, thinking that this big cowboy, in the end, would have to pull in his horns and slink away rather than face two guns—as who wouldn't. The men on the porch kept staring, as if they too expected it.

Part of Fargo's mind had already noted the short distance between the men. When he spoke, his voice was soft. "I think you two are the scummiest hyenas I've ever seen trying to stand up and talk like men."

The street froze into silence.

Johnny and Ray had been smirking, positive the big man would back up. First the shock hit them that he wouldn't. Then the thought hit them he might be a fast gun, and that one of them might go. Their smirks went sick. But everyone was watching— their game had been called. They had to move. Still, one of them might come through unhurt— maybe both. The sweat started on their faces, their mouths twisted. But the stranger waited, his eyes icy.

They went for their guns.

Fargo's move was so fast that his two shots sounded almost like one. Ray never got his gun from his holster; the bullet tore his chest apart. Johnny got his gun out, but Fargo's bullet hit his throat and he grabbed at it, choked, spun to the earth, twisting and twisting, making guttural sounds for a minute before he went still.

Fargo looked at the porch—everyone was frozen, no hostile move. They were looking on death, but never expected such lightning gunplay. Their eyes followed the lean, powerful man walking toward the girl waiting on her black horse.

Julie's eyes were unreadable as they moved to the hotel. She was angry that he'd let himself get sidetracked by two mangy, no-account skunks. And she feared that his foolish call-out of two guns would get him hurt. That, for her, would be a hard blow in her pursuit of vengeance. She needed his

70

trailsmanship to track the killers. For an idle moment he wondered how she would handle it if he was out of the picture. She was driven by a deadly hate and would not stop until she could pay off the men who'd killed her family. But she'd be too clever to confront them straight on; probably she'd try to ambush them, just as she had tried on him.

She looked far away in thought, and his own mood was grim. He felt tight, nervous; the duel with the two men had been ugly. He felt almost nothing about the shoot-out—men like them, drunken and vicious, had done, he knew from experience, a heavy share of killing, and they picked on good people, vulnerable people. They were bullies, and the only reason they'd picked on him was the presence of Julie, and their belief he'd not challenge two guns. Well, he thought with an ironic smile, they got a lesson, but learned it in the few seconds of their death throes.

The hotel lobby was a plain, red room with a small counter behind which a plump, red-faced man dozed in a rickety wicker chair. His iron-gray hair was slicked down, parted in the middle, and he had a puttylike nose on which a giant horsefly had just settled.

Fargo rapped the counter, which didn't disturb the horsefly but did cause the heavy lids of the sleeper to slide open, revealing a pair of light blue eyes. The monster insect on his nose caught his attention and he made a wild swing, which missed but sent the horsefly into a rage, and it circled lightning fast around his head, sounding like a buzz saw before it streaked off.

"Everything's big in Texas," grumbled the man.

"Sorry to disturb your rest," Fargo said, "but we'd like a couple of rooms."

At the thought of business, his glazed eyes suddenly cleared and he grinned, struggled to his feet, rubbed his hands. "Sure, sure—just a bit of a catnap, mister." He pointed to himself. "Amos Beasely, proprietor of the Lone Star Hotel." He glanced at Julie. "Did you say a room or a couple of rooms?"

"Two separate rooms," said Julie firmly.

Fargo glanced at her with amusement. "And the lady would like a bath, if you can arrange it."

The wide mouth spread under the puttylike nose. "Amos Beasely can arrange most things. The rooms are two dollars. The bath two bits. And if you sign the register, we'll be happy to start the water heating for the lady's bath. We also have good eats."

The register was a yellowed notebook with pencil-ruled lines and a few names. Fargo glanced through them. He let Julie climb the stairs to room number 3 and stayed to talk to Beasely.

"I'm looking for two men who go by the names of Joadie and Red, traveling together. Happen to pass through town, would you know?"

A shrewd look came to Beasely's face. "Looking for them, are you?" His eyes slowly examined Fargo, the lean, powerful body, the big Colt.

"I think I said that."

"Not aiming to be hostile, are you, mister?"

Fargo scowled. A joker who ran off at the mouth, but he had to be smart or he wouldn't have reached middle age in a territory where a loose mouth got you a quick funeral.

"Just said I'm looking. Do you know them?"

Amos smiled. "Know what I learned in life, Mr. Fargo? That knowledge is not only power but money. What do you think of that?"

Fargo grimaced. The old varmint was a businessman, and selling information was business. He put a golden eagle on the counter. Beasely's pale blue eyes that looked dopey when his lids first slipped open glittered shrewdly now, and the way the coin disappeared into his pocket was a wonder to behold. "Joadie Smith and Red Logan. They were in town two days. That's a fact." He spoke slowly as if he was thinking a lot.

Fargo studied the round face with its hair slapped flat against the skull. He won't put out unless its squeezed out, he thought. "What can you tell me about them?"

Beasely looked startled at the question, and his shrewd eyes narrowed. "Why do you want to meet them, Mr. Fargo, if I'm not too nosy?"

He was damned nosy. "I want to meet them as a favor for a friend."

Beasely thought for a moment, then he shrugged. "They look like heroes from hell, that's what they look like. And it wouldn't surprise me if their guns have put as many men in hell as the devil himself."

Fargo said nothing, waiting.

"In two days, they had four fights, two in the saloon, two on the street. Killed four men. Joadie has a fast gun, very fast. So, mister, if an old head can advise you, I'd be very careful in my dealings with these men."

Fargo's smile was grim. "I'll keep it in mind.

He went upstairs to a room with a wooden bed and a dresser painted red. He dropped on the bed in his boots, put his hands behind his head, stared at a crack in the ceiling, then his lids came down like lead and soon he was snoring. When he opened his eyes and glanced through the small square window, he saw, to his astonishment, a night sky lit up with moonlight. He must have slept for hours.

He listened for sound from the room next door, Julie's room; heard none. Probably asleep for the night. They'd been hitting it hard on the trail, and if it wore him down, what did it do to her? He could hear sounds on the street, so it couldn't be far into the night. A good time to drop into the saloon, maybe get a better line on Joadie Smith and Red Logan. He clumped down the stairs, saw nobody at the counter. In the street men were laughing, drinking and quarreling.

When he reached the saloon, he could hear the sound of a dinky piano and pushed open the swinging doors. Eight men at the bar, five at the card table and two women near the piano, one playing. The men turned to look as they always did at a stranger, and though the piano still tinkled, the men went silent. There was a bit of whispering and it occurred to Fargo that the word was out on his shooting—in a town like this word would go out like wildfire. The bar had a big silvered mirror and a stack of bottles and a freckle-faced, redheaded bartender with cool gray eyes.

"Whiskey," said Fargo.

One of the cowboys at the bar, with a square face and friendly eyes, spoke. "Mister, I've seen a lot of shooting, but nothing like what I saw this afternoon. You sorta made history in this town. Could I buy you a drink?"

Fargo nodded pleasantly.

"I saw the Dakota Kid once in action," said a tall thin cowboy, "but his hand never moved like yours."

The barman, whom the men called Dundee, watched Fargo with his cool gray eyes. "They planted Johnny and Ray in boot hill. They're better off dead. Bad blood in those two. Two days ago they burned out McCormick and shot him. Because

74

they'd heard he said the town'd be better off without them."

Fargo lifted his glass. The two men had been polecats, just as he had judged—he'd seen too many in the territory not to know the signs.

"Staying in town, mister?" asked Dundee. "We could use a gun like yours to clean up the place."

Fargo smiled. "From the look of it, you need the cavalry." He glanced at the cardplayers, now concentrating on their game under the green-shaded light, then at the two women at the piano. They wore red silk dresses that hugged their bodies and advertised the merchandise. They were plump pigeons and he felt horny, but neither hit him right. He thought of Joadie and Red and turned to the barman, but just then the swinging doors opened and Fargo stopped to stare. The young woman standing there also wore a red silk dress, but the way it fit her was spectacular, and it had to do with the body underneath. The low cut of the dress revealed a jutting pair of breasts, a long slender waist and curving hips. She had fine auburn hair that fell lavishly to her shoulders. Her face was pretty, her skin sleek and her dark brown eyes gleamed cynically. The lips were full, but the mouth had a touch of hardness. Though young, she looked as if she didn't care much for the way life had treated her.

"Hi, Lily," Dundee said, and he couldn't help smiling at Fargo. Fargo realized his mouth had dropped open at the sight of the woman, and it must have looked comic to the barman. Lily nodded to Dundee, glanced at Fargo, at the others in the bar, then came back to Fargo. Her eyes were shrewd and hard.

She sauntered in, looked Fargo squarely in the

eye, a mocking, sexy invitation, then sat at a table alone.

His breathing quickened: he felt primed as a wild stallion, and Lily, with those ripe breasts and bawdy-looking buttocks, was exactly what he wanted. She had a touch of hardness, yes, but what the hell, life wasn't a bed of roses. And Fargo had found that riding with a beautiful woman like Julie kept his juices simmering. But they were on a holy mission; she'd lost her family—you didn't make a sex pitch in a situation like that. Much too bad because he found Julie a feast to the eyes, the way she was, the way she rode, the way she moved, graceful as a cat. Yes, if he could have his druthers, he'd go for Julie like an arrow to its target, but his code blocked him.

He gazed at Lily sitting at the table, her dark eyes fastened on him. "Do I get a drink, cowboy?" she asked.

Dundee's gray eyes were strange as he put down two glasses and a bottle. Fargo took them to her table, wondering what bothered the barman. What the hell did he know about Lily? A dangerous woman? Maybe yes, maybe no. It all went out of his mind when he sat at the table with Lily; her body radiated such physical presence it blotted out everything. The nipples of her breasts stuck against her dress like arrow tips and her sleek flesh seemed to glow as if fed by a sex fire underneath. "Thanks." She lifted her drink, tossed it off, and motioned for him to refill it.

Then she threw a glance toward the women. "Give us a tune, Ruby."

One of the plump pigeons sat on the piano stool and began a sweet waltz. The piano had a couple of sour notes, but it wasn't half bad and the tune was romantic.

"When'd you hit town?" she asked.

"Early today."

"What's the name?"

"Fargo, Skye Fargo."

She nodded. "Was it you who did the fast shooting this morning and did in poor Johnny Slade and Ray?" Somehow she seemed to know it was him, and he wondered why she asked.

"A couple of stinking hyenas," he said.

Her eyebrows lifted. "They said the wrong thing to your girl—was that it?"

"They said the wrong thing to the lady I was traveling with."

"And you shot them? That's hard, isn't it?"

His eyes narrowed. "Friends of yours, those two?"

Her face was masklike. "I knew them. When they drank, they got out of hand. Like a lotta men." ,

He stroked his chin. "A man is responsible for what he says."

Her eyes glittered and she seemed bothered by her thoughts. "You ask a lot from people, Fargo."

He squinted at her. She seemed to have a kind word for the rattlesnakes. "Don't understand why you defend them. They were killers. I can smell a killer."

"Can you? What kind of smell, Fargo?" Her smile was cynical and her eyes weren't friendly. He fingered his glass and began to wonder if it'd be better to forget about Lily and bedtime. She might look like sex dynamite, but she talked in a way that started a chill in him: in fact, he was going cold as a brass donkey in a Dakota freeze. Too bad, because the sight of her had put his pants in an uproar.

She sensed his mood change, then softened, aware

that she'd pushed him too hard. "It doesn't matter, does it—just two killers less in the world?" she said, and turned on the sex again, which hit him like a heat wave: she smiled, her skin seemed to glow, her mouth moved with erotic promise. "Let's have a party, Fargo, how about it? Just bring the bottle." And she stood, walked to the stairs. He watched the move of her buttocks, pure music, and sighed. He followed her up the stairs to a room with a low wooden bed, a red cotton spread, a yellow dresser with a basin of water, an oval mirror on the wall.

When the door shut behind him, she turned and started to unbutton his jeans. For a woman who, only minutes ago, threw ice chips at him, she'd suddenly turned into one hot lady. She brought him out and he looked swollen with desire. Her eyes widened at the sight, and whatever else lurked in her mind seemed lost in the way she went about her business. She kissed, fondled, loved it, her hand moving up and down on it with brazen lust. Then she stopped and, in a frenzy, threw off her clothing; her body looked just as promised by the outline of her dress. The skin was satiny, the breasts and hips voluptuous. At the nook between her thighs the hair had been scissored thin and her scarlet lips peeped. He was seething. His mouth moved to her breasts, his hands to the round, silky buttocks. He stroked her, finding great pleasure in the curves of her body; he took her to bed where she sat down and again brought his bigness to her. Her lips parted and her appetite for loving seemed insatiable; he could scarcely pull away, her craving seemed so urgent until, finally, unable to hold off, he exploded, and she held him firm, engulfing him.

He dropped on the bed and stared at the ceiling.

She lay beside him and watched him with a curious smile. He went dreamy for a time, then opened his eyes. She still lay beside him, eyes open, looking thoughtful. He gazed at her body, the beautiful breasts, the softly rounded stomach, and felt again the surge of desire. He looked down; definite sign of life.

She had turned at his movement and smiled at his sexual agitation. "Answer to a maiden's dream," she drawled.

He slipped over her silky body, felt its curves, pushed apart her thighs, and slipped into the juicy warmth. A sigh escaped her, as if the sensation was unexpected. He held her smooth buttocks and began to move, slowly, trying to get every moment of pleasure, then feeling the rising tension, he put speed to his movements until he was pounding against her body. As he drove he felt a great pulsation of pleasure, he felt her body coming up to meet his, heard her gasps. He drove on and on and her grip tightened on his body, and she let out a cry, as if she'd been shocked at her feelings. As for him, his passion spiraled and he pumped savagely until the final overpowering surge.

As they lay side by side, later, it occurred to him that a woman like her could be a good source of news. "You hear about things, Lily, right? Things around town."

She turned, lifted her eyebrows. "Like what?"

He put his hands behind his head. "Tell you—I'm looking for a couple of men—Joadie Smith and Red Logan. Happen to know where I can find them?" He glanced at her.

Again that curious smile. "Well, Fargo, about two

79

hours ago, I might have told you. But not now, not anymore."

His eyes opened. "What do you mean?" He lifted himself on his elbow. "Are they in town?" Beasely never said that!

"Oh yes, they were in town."

"And now?"

"Who would know, Fargo?"

He stared; it never occurred to him they might be in town, and the fact that they were made his hackles rise. Why did Beasely give the impression they were not in town?

He looked at her. "How do you know they're gone?"

"Just a feeling. Maybe it's because you're in town." Her lids slid down and it made him sit up. This girl seemed to know a helluva lot. He thought a bit. "Tell me, did you know I was looking for them?"

"How would I know that?" She was looking at him with her cynical eyes.

He put his feet on the floor. "How in hell did they know I was looking?"

Her mouth twisted in a curious smile. "Maybe you were doing too much asking around, that's how."

He digested that. Back in Little Creek and here, at the hotel, he had done the asking. Would word get around that fast! He gazed at her. "Since you know so much, where'd they go?"

She just shook her head. He dressed fast. "Lily, tell me, what the hell is in the back of your mind?" She baffled hell out of him. She knew something and was holding on to it. And it was locked into the men he was tracking. Were they nearby, waiting, outside the room? He'd have heard them. Downstairs? No, he believed, as she had said, that they'd left town. Why? Even if he'd done some fast

80

shooting, they didn't seem to be men who'd run. More the type who'd want to pit themselves against him.

Lily, who'd been watching him, spoke. "What about this girl you're traveling with. Why'd you come with me, when you had her, Fargo?"

His eyes were cold. "I don't have her. I told you, we're traveling together, that's all."

"You don't have her," Lily repeated, her smile mocking, and something in her tone jolted him. Maybe she was shooting words, but whether she meant it or not, she'd put a burr in his brain. He wanted to shake her and squeeze out what she knew. But he thought about Julie. Abruptly, he stood up, dropped a golden eagle on the dresser, threw her a hard look and went out. His body was nerved up to expect anything, but the stairway was empty, and nobody waited for him outside the saloon. He moved fast up the street, his eye quick to search the doorways and shadows. He didn't in the least like the idea that Joadie and Red had been in town and that Beasely had not told it. Beasely, that mangy dog, had given him the idea they'd gone. It wouldn't be smart for Beasely to be standing around just now. Why, he wondered, did Beasely, a proper citizen, favor men like those two killer dogs. A mystery. But a man who'd sell information to you would sell it elsewhere, just as quick.

As he expected, Beasely was not at the counter, just a lad of sixteen who whittled at a slingshot. He glanced at Fargo with a dull eye and went back to whittling. Fargo climbed the stairs, feeling something wrong. He sensed it, a tingly, jittery feeling along his nerves. He pulled his gun, moved silently to his door, kicked it open. Nothing. He moved to Julie's door, quietly turning the knob, pushed it softly. Empty! She'd been in her bed and sleeping, but the bed was empty, the cover thrown back, her clothes gone. He studied the floor marks with a scowl. Then he went down the stairs, stopped, put a hard eye on the lad. He was a blond youngster with long hair, fair skin. He'd heard the door kicked in and looked nervous.

"Where's Beasely?"

"Dunno, sir. Hope he gets back soon, 'cause I gotta go home. Gettin' late."

"The lady in room three, where'd she go?"

The boy looked bewildered. "Dunno." His voice quavered.

Fargo leaned toward him; he'd seen scuff marks on the floor of her room. "What happened, boy, talk straight."

The boy gulped, obviously scared. "Joadie Smith came in, told me to go into the back room and shut the door. Then he went upstairs. That's all I know. I came out fifteen minutes later, long after he'd come down. Didn't see anything. Don't know what happened."

The boy was telling the truth, Fargo decided, and walked to the front of the hotel, examined the ground carefully. The moon shone brightly and he could trace the deep scuff marks of a man's boot, heavy because of his burden. Fresh hoof marks of two horses moving east. He studied the markings, locked them in his memory, then went to the porch of the hotel, sat in the rickety wicker chair. He needed to think because a lot was going on, a lot that had to be figured out.

First Joadie Smith and Red Logan, the two killers he hadn't yet seen, had known he was in town, that he was looking for them. How'd they know? Word coming from Little Creek, where he knocked off their pal, Bowie? Or from Beasely, a man who'd peddle his mother for dollars? That could be why Beasely took a powder, to lie low till Fargo left town or got himself killed. Joadie came to the hotel, not to call him out—he'd have done that at the saloon—but to carry Julie off. But to do that he had to be sure that Fargo'd be out of the way. *That's where Lily came in.* She had appeared at the saloon *after* he walked in, hadn't she? Her job was to nail him down. But she'd talked too much, couldn't help it. What else did she know? What about Red; where was he? Why hadn't he come with Joadie to the hotel? Lily might have a few answers. He'd better find out before he started tracking Joadie. Why did she cooperate with scum like that? What kind of power did Joadie and Red have? Even Beasely, what made him play on their team? The power of the gun? It might be something else, and that was the mystery. Why'd they take Julie? Did they know it was her family they'd killed? How'd they know that? They knew she was traveling with him and that he was looking for them. He couldn't get a handle on it, not yet; he stood up and started to the saloon.

The moon gleamed silver in the windows of the storefronts on Main Street.

"Where's Lily?" he asked Dundee in a soft voice.

Dundee came to the corner of the bar. "Not here, Fargo. Gone." His gray eyes were clouded.

"Where'd she go?" Fargo asked, his voice hard.

Dundee reached under the bar and brought up a sheet of paper. "She left this note in case you wanted to know."

Fargo glanced at the note. Her penmanship was awful.

Fargo: I've left town. It'd be a waste of time to come after me. You'd be smart to go back where you came from. It's a warning. Lily.

Fargo stared at Dundee, who had poured himself a drink. "You know Joadie and Red?"

The barman nodded. "They came here."

"What the hell did they have on Lily?"

Dundee stroked his chin. "Joadie and Lily got something going on between them—thick as thieves."

"They are? What about Red?"

Dundee lifted his whiskey and drank it. "Tell you, Fargo. Joadie and Red are a couple of very tough men. They also have powerful connections—back in Waco."

"What connections?"

"Don't ask me. It's just whispered around. Nobody really knows. You won't get any more than that in this town."

"Gimme a whiskey," Fargo said, and pushed his hat back on his head. He too doubted that he'd get anything more out of this town. It'd be better to hightail east. Somehow he didn't believe Joadie would put violent hands on Julie. It was Julie who might trigger the violence, considering how she felt about the killers of her family. Joadie must have knocked her cold or tied her up to get her out of that hotel. She couldn't know who he was when he barged into her room.

Fargo looked at Dundee. "And what about Red Logan, where's he?"

Dundee's gray eyes stayed on Fargo. "I've got a feeling that if you find Red, you're gonna find Lily too."

Fargo grimaced: of course, the bitch nailed him down with sex while Joadie grabbed Julie. Red waited for Lily, and right now they were racing to join up with Joadie. That had to be it.

He drank his whiskey, nodded at Dundee, put a piece on the counter and went through the swinging doors.

Outside, the big moon laid a paint of silver over the town.

Fifteen minutes later, he was out on the trail, following the fresh prints of two pairs of horses.

The trail was clear and twisted southeast. The full moon glared down on the earth, throwing brilliant light on a great cluster of pines. The shadows were heavy, especially around the boulders and trees, and more than once Fargo slowed down to make sure no danger lurked in the dark depths. His ear picked up the night sounds, a skulking coyote, a scrabbling marmot, the hoot of an owl, the cry of a nighthawk. And his eye never stopped reading the prints of the trail: the heavy and light prints of Joadie and Julie's horses, and after them, the prints left by Red and Lily.

He wondered if these gunmen might know of his reputation as the Trailsman, and knowing that, would not be setting up camp too soon, fearful that he could barrel down on them. No, they'd push hard, get a big lead before they'd settle for the night. But he still had the edge; he was one, and "he travels fastest who travels alone." Still, they had fresh horses and wouldn't hesitate to put the hard spur to them. He too had to push hard or lose priceless ground.

Did they grab Julie, he wondered, to punish him for Bowie? Or did they have a more sinister idea in mind? It was a damned thing, but the pinto had already done its running most of the day, and powerful as he was, he too must have rest and food. He'd ride two more hours, bed down, be up at dawn and push on.

The brilliant moon made the going easy and his eyes restlessly probed all the darkest shadows and the trail signs. The great pines stood shoulder to shoulder, sending out a tart scent, and every so often a small night animal, startled at the beat of hooves, would scramble madly for the underbrush, as if it expected a murderous attack. Behind the silhouette of the trees Fargo glimpsed the great mountain, a giant profile of rock facing heaven, shrouded in silver and mystery.

He rode another hour, then, aware that the pinto was beginning to strain, he swung off the saddle and walked the horse until he found a good cover, a large boulder in a cozy nook. He threw his bedroll, curried the pinto, turned him loose to graze. The moon had swung toward the horizon and the shadows stretched deeper and darker.

He lay down, put his gun near his hand, as he always did nights on the trail; his lids felt leaden, his bones weary. He shut his eyes.

He'd been sleeping, yes, but how long he didn't know, and didn't look at the moon to judge the time lapse because a danger signal had alerted his body. Something was wrong. Something in the dark, nearby, threatening. He froze: to listen, to locate the sound, even to coax it into movement. Something human was near, trying to get nearer, with deadly intent. An animal? No, his instinct was rarely wrong, and it was silently telling him the threat of instant death was near. No sound, as if the thing out there knew suddenly its quarry had become conscious. Fargo in his mind pictured the position of his gun, let his lids slide open a bit, and the world rushed in on him: the moon still full, the shadows still deep, the boulder behind him big and bulking. But the shape of the boulder was *distorted*. And with that realization, his hand moved with blinding speed to his gun and he twisted away as the human form flung itself at him, knife glinting in the moonlight, raised for the kill. Fargo's bullet hit the body in midair and it came down limp, almost lifeless, just brushing Fargo as it struck the earth.

The man had been hit in the chest but was not dead, not yet. Fargo looked at him, his gun ready to shoot again: a muscular Comanche brave with a blunt thick face, his head shaved. He was breathing painfully and wouldn't last long.

Fargo looked at him, amazed. Why had this Comanche come at him like this? In the middle of the night, as if he had some personal grievance. Indians almost never attacked at night. Why then? Did he just stumble on a white man and feel such hatred he had to destroy him? A sound came from behind the trees, the sound of hoofbeats on the run. Damn, there had been another Comanche. And he got away. No point in pursuit, not at this time of night. He dropped to the Indian, whose breathing came in harsh uneven gasps. Blood leaked from his chest. He'd be gone soon.

Fargo came close to him.

"Why do you make war on Fargo?" he had to ask the question, though he knew that some Indians made war on every white man.

The redskin ignored him, struggled for breath, aware that he was dying. Then, as if some idea came to comfort him, he turned his black, hate-filled eyes up to Fargo. "You have killed Red Wolf, our comrade. The Comanche will kill you." Then he turned away, his lips tight, his face stern, and that's how he died.

Fargo's mind was in a whirl. He'd shot Red Wolf, their great warrior. They'd keep after him until they had their revenge or they gave up the pursuit. It meant they'd track him relentlessly, as long as he was on the trail.

He sighed and looked at the heavens. The moon was sliding down the sky, still three hours to dawn. Damn, in the last twenty-four hours, he'd shot Johnny Slade and Ray, made love to Lily, pursued a kidnapper, knocked off a Comanche.

Well, it hadn't been a dull day.

5

He was up at dawn but felt groggy, he'd been short-changed on sleep. After coffee everything seemed to improve. The pinto looked fresh and power was back in his stride. The sky turned pink; then the sun, huge and orange, came up, scalding the sky before becoming light blue. The land for a time turned flat and the sun-bleached grass stretched far. In the clear air the mountain looked massive and its jagged peaks jabbed at the sky. He stopped at a small twisting stream to let the pinto drink, filled his canteens, swabbed his sweating body. He look back at the sheltering cottonwoods, scrutinized them for movement. The Comanche, the one that had run off, was skulking in there, waiting for his chance, Fargo felt sure. His smile was ironic when he thought how the Comanche trailed him, while he trailed Red and Lily, Joadie and Julie.

A flutter of white in the bushes hit the periphery of his eye. His gun barked and the rabbit fell still. He ate the fried meat with fried bread quickly. It had to be eat and run because the prints of Red and Lily, so damned fresh, told him he was hot on their heels.

Now the trail twisted into rocky ground and the going slowed up. Alongside the trail, the crags piled up on a high slope; he could get a fine overview from there. He tethered the pinto, took his rifle because he never knew what he might find and began to climb. He went up slowly, over crags set steeply, one on top of the other; it was like climbing a ladder. When he got past an obscuring ledge of stone, the view was dazzlingly clear. He was startled to see two people round a campfire, Lily sitting, a redheaded man standing, both drinking coffee. They were just beyond his rifle range, and, anyway, he had no intention of shooting Red. The last thing he wanted was a dead Red, at least not until the man had done some talking about what happened to Julie's family at Eagle Butte.

It was his first sight of Red Logan, and he thought of Beasely's words about Joadie and Red: "They look like heroes out of hell." Red was tall, rangy, with a dark face scarred by knife fights and bullets, and even from that distance, Fargo could see the mouth in a cruel line. Lily, next to him, had changed into a blue shirt and brown riding jeans.

Red, when he raised his cup to drink, suddenly froze, for Fargo came into his sight. Struck by the fixity of his gaze, Lily turned to look, and her hand went to her breast.

For one long moment the three stared at each other, then Red figured that Fargo had done no shooting either because he was out of range or he didn't want him dead. That Fargo wanted him alive to know what he knew, and Red wasn't sticking around for that. He spoke to Lily, and slowly, deliberately, they started for their horses grazing nearby.

Fargo raised his rifle but couldn't touch the trigger. He couldn't be accurate, and a wandering bullet could shut Red's mouth. No, he'd let them go because he knew he'd shortly pick them up again.

They were two and he was one, with the fastest horse in the territory. He didn't have to worry; in fact, he might even let them go through Lemon Creek and pick them up east of it. He watched them swing over their horses and gallop around the curve in the trail and out of sight.

As he started down he considered it wouldn't be long before he'd have Red nailed down and spilling his guts. He picked his way over the slippery crags, once sliding on his tail because of his hurry. When he reached the pinto, he stuck the rifle into its holster and swung over the saddle.

The sun was slamming down heat, and when he reached the next sparkling rivulet, he stopped to let the pinto drink, wiped his sweaty body and neck, keeping a wary eye behind him for the tenacious redskin.

When he mounted up and chugged along the trail, no longer in a hurry, he couldn't help chuckle as he remembered Red's shocked expression as he looked up the cliff. He must have figured he'd be dead if Fargo didn't have a special reason for not shooting. What he knew was keeping him alive.

As Fargo looked down at the racing prints of his quarry he couldn't help speculate on how much Lily knew. She and Joadie, according to the barman, Dundee, had been thick as thieves, real lovers. So, she must know something. How deep was she in all this? Something to think about, wasn't it?

As he rode toward Lemon Creek the sun was a yellow glare in a copper sky. From a high slope, he could see the town, a gathering of ramshackle houses, baking in the shimmering heat. He didn't figure on nailing Red in a place like this unless ambush was on his mind. Not likely; he'd pick up provisions,

91

grab a couple of whiskeys at the saloon and race out.

The way Fargo figured it, Red and Lily had laid out a meeting place with Joadie somewhere in Fort Worth. Why? Because it was big and bustling, and you could pull a couple of rascal stunts in places like that.

The blistering sun put a sweat on the pinto's flanks, but just ahead, about a half mile from town, a big oak spread its branches and leaves. A huge, sturdy tree and its coolness had already enticed three cowboys to its shade.

The trail meandered past the oak and Fargo thought it might be a good idea to stop for cooldown and ask the cowboys if they'd seen his quarry ride by.

The men lolled about, talking, showing no interest in his approach. Their horses, also sweaty, grazed nearby in a rich patch of grass.

Fargo couldn't put a brand on these cowboys; their duds were smart and they looked hefty, beefy, probably workers for a cattle ranch nearby.

As he rode closer they became more attentive to him, something he expected because his Ovaro was such a great-looking animal. Connoisseurs of horseflesh always threw an admiring eye on the Ovaro. He intended to stop, which would give them a still better look.

He pulled up, nodded. "That's a great piece of horseflesh you got there, mister," said a round-faced, brown-eyed, smiling man in a light blue shirt.

"The best there is," Fargo said, and felt kindly toward him, as he did to anyone who admired his pinto.

"One hot day, isn't it?" said the smiling man. "You been doing a lotta riding, cowboy?"

"Just came out of Pottsville," Fargo said, pulling off the pinto and reaching for his canteen. "How far to Lemon Creek?"

"Just about a mile, over the wooden bridge. They've got a good saloon and cold beer. Just right for a thirsty man. Burt's the name."

Fargo nodded; he wouldn't mind a couple of beers on a day like this. He put the canteen back on the saddle. "Fargo," he said. The other two men were studying the Ovaro with obvious interest.

"Run into any redskin trouble out there?" Burt asked.

"They're out there. I'd be careful, traveling west."

"Just a couple of wild young bucks," said one of the cowboys. Burt moved toward the pinto, to examine him.

"I'm looking," Fargo said, "for a big redheaded man and a lady who might have gone through here in the last few hours. Any of you men happen to see them?"

There was a moment of silence, then Fargo turned to look at Burt and found himself looking into a gun. Burt said nothing for a moment, then spoke in a friendly voice. "Just pull your Colt up with two fingers on the handle and drop it. Slowly, like a nice fella."

Fargo stared hard at him. "Are you sure you got the right man, mister?"

Burt cocked his gun. "I suppose I might shoot you right off—you don't have to drop your gun."

Fargo lifted his Colt with his fingers and dropped it, staring. "Now, what's it about, mister?"

The three men studied him, and he could tell they meant nothing good.

"It's about the little lady called Lily," the smiling Burt said. "We were waiting for you, Fargo."

Fargo scowled. What the hell was going on. What cock-and-bull story did they get from Lily? Whatever it was, the men seemed to have swallowed all of it. They looked ready to be ugly.

"Yeah, Fargo, we were waiting under this tree to give you a real pain in the neck." The other men laughed, and one of them pulled the pinto toward the grass patch. "Get the rope, Tom." And a beefy, red-faced, barrel-chested man with a crooked smile started toward his horse for the rope. As he passed Fargo he grinned. "Yeah, we're going to string you up for what you did to Lily."

Fargo's eyes narrowed. "I think you men got a bum steer. I did nothing to Lily."

"Nothing but rape, hey, Fargo," said Burt. "Well, we know how to handle rapists around here."

Fargo felt a chill in his gut. These goddamn idiots didn't know Lily was a whore, and were ready to take her word and swing him. And it could happen in the next couple of minutes unless he talked them out of it.

"What did Lily say I did—I got a right to know."

"C'mon, Burt, don't waste time," Tom said; he had the rope and seemed to have a taste for hanging. His crooked mouth twisted as if he was about to have good fun.

Fargo took a deep breath. "Listen, Burt, even in this territory a man has a right to know the crime he's accused of."

"Tell him, Burt," said the third man, who had dark small eyes and a lantern jaw. "He's going to hell, let him have something to think about on the way."

"You think so, Scotty?" Burt, stony-faced, turned to Fargo. "Lily says you crept up on them while they were camping. Got the drop on Red, tied him up, then forced yourself on her. You got to be a lowdown polecat—even hanging's too good for you."

Fargo shook his head. It was hard to believe that any level-headed man would swallow a story like that from a woman like Lily. "It's a lie, Burt. The woman's a whore—ask anyone in Pottsville."

Tom swung and hit Fargo on the cheek; he tasted blood. "You got a dirty mouth, Fargo. But we'll shut it for you—permanent."

Burt's face was grim, but under it was a strange smile. "You talk real ugly, mister. But it don't matter."

To Fargo, the situation didn't make sense. He had moved from the hunter to the prey in the space of minutes; actually he'd run into an ambush just as if Red and Lily were pointing guns.

"Just don't rush it, Burt. Give a man a chance to prove he's telling the truth."

"What truth? Saying you didn't put your hands on Lily?" Tom had thrown the rope over a sturdy branch and it came down near Fargo's head. Every muscle in Fargo's body tensed. "I told you, she's a saloon girl, out of Pottsville. Why isn't she here if she's got something to say?"

Burt just smiled that strange smile and watched Tom making the noose.

Then Fargo realized that these men had come to hang and do nothing else. Somehow Red and Lily had got to them and they didn't care if Fargo was as innocent as a newborn babe. Whatever the reason, whether it was money or something else, they never for a moment believed Lily was a lady whose purity had been violated by Fargo.

It was a desperate moment and unless he could think of something in the next minutes, they'd have him dangling from that tree. The threat of death speeded his flow of thought. It was either getting hung or getting shot if he made a break. Tom was bringing the noose close to his head and within moments would throw it over his neck. And there was Burt in front of him, the gun pointing at his heart. And Scotty, the lantern jaw, was just standing and looking.

Damn, was he finished, was it all going to end like this? Near this blister of a town, lynched by three rotten hyenas?

His gaze swung around; nobody was near, it was outside the edge of town, the site had been picked carefully. The ground was clear, except for a clump of bushes off to his right.

So there was no help; he'd have to make his move, probably take a bullet from Burt, hoping it would not hit a vital spot and that he could still do some damage to these scum.

"Go ahead, Tom," Burt said, pointing with his gun at the tree. It was then Fargo heard the whoosh, a sound he understood instantly, even before he heard the thunk as the arrow hit Burt in the heart. Burt reeled back, his eyes in shock, his gun firing, the bullet hitting the ground. Everyone was paralyzed, then lightning quick, Fargo grabbed Tom, swung behind him, one hand pinning him, the other grabbing his gun, which, in one move, he pulled and fired into Tom's body, holding the sagging figure in front of him as Scotty tried to get a bullet off. Fargo fired again and Scotty staggered back with a hole in his chest. Fargo went into a crouch and stared at the clump of bushes from where the arrow had come. Nothing, no sign of movement. The Comanche had saved him, not out of love but because, if Fargo was to die, it must be by the hand of the Comanche, not by the ugly paleface. Fargo stayed crouched, not to tempt the Comanche with a target. He glanced at Burt lying there, the arrow deep in his heart, his shirt wet with blood. The gun had dropped from his hand and he was going fast.

Fargo leaned close and whispered. "Hey, Burt, come clean before you go. Why'd you do this?"

Burt struggled for breath, looked at Fargo; he seemed to have trouble recognizing him, he was sinking fast. Then a light gleamed in the dull eyes and he flicked his finger. Fargo leaned close to his mouth. "Tell Lee," then he died.

Tell Lee? Who the hell was Lee? Tell him what? He had something on his mind that he never got off. Fargo shrugged and looked around: three dead men, and in the bushes a deadly Comanche. This was no place to loiter. These, he felt, were not local men; they came from somewhere else, but he didn't intend to lose precious time to find out. He should go through Lemon Creek like a dose of salts through a wildcat, and try to pick up Red and Lily up the trail. His jaw tightened; they had played dirty pool and the anger he felt about them burned hot. He looked again toward the bushes; he'd keep low, use the trunk of the tree for cover. He crawled toward the pinto. His feeling for the Comanche was gratitude; he understood of course the Comanche intended his death, but didn't want anyone else to usurp that pleasure. But Fargo would rather take chances in a one-to-one with a Comanche than with three slimy polecats who'd just got their deserved reward.

He swung over his horse, crouched low, put the horse into a gallop and waved his hand to his unseen benefactor.

*   *   *

He followed Red's track into town, through its main street, hot, dusty, its storefronts made of rough logs painted brown. Red's prints stopped at Johnson's General Store, and Fargo, on impulse, went in.

Johnson was a bald, stout man with a jowly face and an apron worn up to his armpits. Fargo ordered beef jerky, cans of beans and oats.

"Yessir," Johnson said, smiling genially, and as he filled the order he glanced curiously at Fargo. "Going through?"

Fargo nodded.

"Lotta traffic going through today, and it's still early."

"Like who?" Fargo asked as if making conversation.

"Three men came up from east Texas, a big man and a woman. Now you. That's a lot of traffic for a town like Lemon Creek. It's a good town, mister. Good farming soil, good cattle country. If you're looking to settle, this is a good place."

Fargo smiled faintly. Settling was the last thought in his mind. "The man and woman who went through—how long ago was that?"

Johnson frowned. "Not that long. She was one good-looking woman. More curves to her than on a dancing snake."

Fargo thought of Lily in bed. She had curves all right. "Say where they were headed?" If he knew that, he would cut time. They may have felt that Burt's lynch gang would stop him and that they didn't have to hide anything.

"Naw, didn't say. They went east. Bought enough to get them to Fort Worth." He examined Fargo. "Lawman, are you?"

"No." He smiled as he picked up his provisions. He wasn't a lawman, but he sure liked to see justice done, and whenever he could, he put his gun on the side of justice.

Out on the brown dirt street, the sun hammered down hard, and he rode the pinto easy until he came out to the trail. He could tell from the hoofprints that Red no longer felt threatened from behind. His pace was leisurely.

Now the land became sandy, with sparse vegetation, land where snakes and lizards crawled in the sun. Overhead a buzzard circled lazily, waiting for the inevitable dinner below. Fargo stopped for the pinto to drink twice, pouring water from his canteen into his hat. It was dry, scorched land that reflected a harsh, cruel sun and it took hours to get through, to reach timbered land.

From the prints, he could tell he'd picked up time on Red. Thinking of him, his face hardened. Red was in for a brutal surprise. He thought there had been a necktie party in Lemon Creek and wouldn't expect to get hit in the middle of the country. It was now grassy, hilly with shrubs and trees. Fargo knew that shortly he'd pick up Red and Lily. He'd come down on them from the slope, put a couple of nails in Red to make him talk.

Just then he felt the sting on his left arm, after that the bark of a rifle. He cursed, dropped from the pinto as if he'd been dead hit and rolled in the tall grass.

The flesh high on his left arm had been nicked; it would bleed a little then clot. Could have been worse, except he'd been a moving target and Red was no sharpshooter. That's what came from wool-gathering on the trail, a fatal disease. He had figured that Red, believing him lynched, wouldn't take the time to climb a slope and look back. But he did. Why? Maybe Burt was supposed to race up and tell him the lynching had been done. But Burt never came. So Red stopped to look and to his amazement saw Fargo coming on big as life. It so excited him, he shot fast and almost missed.

What would he do now? Sit behind that small boulder on the slope, from where he had to shoot, wait for his target to bleed and weaken, then go in?

Fargo studied the terrain. His job was to get behind Red, not a hard thing; there was tall grass, shrubs and tree trunks for cover.

He crawled for twenty yards, circled wide, came up in a crouch, moved up high on the slope. Down below he could see Red with his rifle, peering at the spot where the pinto grazed. He was chafing. Fargo smiled: Red didn't know if he'd hit his target or not, and didn't know what to do—wait or go in.

Fargo came down slowly, crawling through the tall grass, his descent noiseless. He paused to study the ground. No sign of Lily, where the hell did Red put her before he embarked on his ambush? He'd find out, soon enough. Over the tall grass he could see Red's black flat hat, the black neckerchief, the broad shoulders.

"Don't move or you're dead," Fargo said.

Red froze, then cursed.

"Take the rifle by its barrel, slow, that's right. Now fling it."

The rifle sailed off into the bushes.

Fargo stepped in front of Red, plucked the gun from his holster. Red was big all right, with blue eyes, high cheeks, with fist-and-knife scars on his face. His neck was thick. It was a cruel face, the face of a man who made his living by his gun.

"Well, Red, I've been wanting to meet you."

Red looked surly. "Never cared to meet you, I must say."

Fargo smiled sourly. "That's wasn't a nice trick you pulled on me—back in Lemon Creek."

Red was silent.

"You tried to get me lynched, because I raped Lily." He laughed. "That had to be a joke—raping a woman like Lily. Stealing her virtue."

Red's face, though grim, loosened a bit; he seemed to appreciate the irony.

"Why'd you do that, Red?"

Red grumbled. "You been stickin' to us like glue. Seemed a good way to get loose of you."

"But how'd you talk that gang into trying it—lynch an innocent man?"

"You ain't innocent, Fargo. You're butting into something that's not your business."

Fargo's jaw clenched. "What happened to Julie is my business."

Red shrugged. "You're making one big mistake, Fargo. You're up against something bigger than you know."

"Yeah?" Fargo walked in front of him. "How big? What do you know about it? Come clean, Red, and I'll give you a fair fighting shot."

"Whaddya mean? Draw on you—that's not fair fighting. We heard how you took Johnny Slade and Ray—at one time. I'm no match for you. I won't draw. You'd have to kill me in cold blood."

Fargo studied him; the bastard seemed to mean it.

"Where's Lily?" he asked.

Red shrugged.

Fargo swung, hit Red in the mouth and he staggered. Blood sprang from his lip. He glared, but said nothing.

Fargo drew his fist back again. Red spoke quickly.

"Up the trail, 'bout half a mile, in a cabin, waiting for me."

"Waiting for you. Let's you go there. Not nice to keep a lady of virtue waiting."

It was a line cabin built of rough logs, used to keep range cowboys protected from harsh weather in winter. Fargo made Red approach from the rear, and when Red opened the door he followed in close behind.

There was a table, bench and a wooden bed; Lily was resting on the bed. She gaped at Fargo, her eyes big. In spite of being a little rattlesnake, she had, he thought, one helluva body lying there, and he couldn't help feeling a sting of desire looking at her. He shook off the feeling.

Lily's eyes burned at Red. "You worm. Can't you do anything right? And why'd you have to bring him here?"

"Aw shut up," Red growled. There seemed to be bad blood between them, something that surfaced traveling together, Fargo surmised.

She bit her lip in anger. "Not much of a man are you? You go out to get him, and instead, bring him back here. I told Joadie you had no balls."

Red glared at her murderously. "You slut. I wish you had balls for one minute. I'd beat you to a pulp."

She goaded him. "That's right. Just like a yellow-belly to want to fight a woman."

Fargo listened with pleasure; it was good strategy to let them beat each other's heads.

But they seemed to have emptied their venom, and fell silent, still glowering.

"Well, now that I've got you lovebirds together," Fargo said pleasantly, "I want the lowdown on this whole operation." He turned to Red. "How'd you

102

happen to hit the Davis family in Eagle Butte, Red?"

Red looked sullenly out the window as if hoping someone would come along and pull him out of this hole.

Fargo backed off, raised his gun. "I'll count to three; if you don't start talking, I'm going to pick pieces off you."

Lily's mouth hardened. "Don't say a word, Red. He won't do it."

Fargo smiled at her. "Burt wanted to hang me, Lily, for raping you. I don't like to be reminded of that. Might want to pay you off." He turned back to Red, pointed his gun.

"I'll ask again—why'd you wipe out the Davis family in Eagle Butte?"

Again a long silence.

Fargo thought of how the woman and boy looked on the cabin floor, facedown, in a big pool of blood.

He fired.

Red yelled, grabbed the side of his shoulder where a piece of flesh had been ripped. He looked at his hand, it was bloody.

"Damn you, Fargo."

Lily's eyes glittered dangerously. Fargo didn't like it. "Move in front of me, lady of virtue, where I can see you good. Move!"

Lily dragged a few steps forward, her face twisted in an ugly grimace. "Are you going to shoot me too? Big brave man."

His gaze, ice cold, went back to Red. "Once again, Red." And he raised his gun.

Red groaned. "Hold it, Fargo. All I know is that Joadie wanted me and Bowie to do a job in Eagle Butte. Said there'd be three hundred dollars each for us, and we'd keep what we found in the house. Supposed to be big money there."

Fargo's eyes squinted curiously. "Why'd he want to hit that particular family?"

Red shrugged, looked at Lily.

"Whyn't you leave him alone?" Lily said through clenched teeth. She seemed more upset than Red.

Fargo brought up his gun.

Red began to talk. "I don't know, but Bowie said somebody wanted Joadie to do the job. Hired him for it."

"Red!" Lily's voice was threatening.

Fargo scowled. "Hired him? Who hired him?"

Red shook his head. "Don't know. That's honest."

Fargo studied the dark eyes; he seemed to be telling the truth. Fargo sat on the edge of the table. "Those men in Lemon Creek, at the tree. Where'd they come from? And how'd you talk them into a lynch party?"

Red shook his head. "Joadie sent them. Surprised me, much as it did you. They'd come to help. Rode in from . . ."

Too late Fargo saw the derringer in Lily's hand. She had bent to pull her stockings and the tiny pistol came out and barked once. Red went down.

Fargo's hand streaked out, grabbed the gun from her fingers and flung her against the wall. She went down like a pole. He leaned to Red: it was a death wound, hit right in the chest, the bright blood pumped out.

"That filthy slut," he whispered. "Shoulda shot her long ago."

Fargo held his head. "You're finished, Red. Might as well talk. Who hired Joadie? Where'd the men come from?"

Red's eyes were clouding. "Somebody . . . in Waco . . ." He stared over at Lily, then his eyes went blank.

104

6

Lily lay flat on her tail against the wall. He'd slammed her hard and she may have dented her head. He stared at her lying there. She had tried to get him lynched, she had stalled him on a bed, so that Joadie could grab Julie, and she had just killed Red.

In short, she was an eighteen-carat bitch, everything he despised, and if she'd been a man, he'd have blasted her the moment she shot Red. But she was a woman, and he couldn't put a bullet in that beautiful body. What made it more idiotic, he got horny just looking at her on the floor—that body, those jutting tits and rounded hips.

What made Lily so vicious? It had to be Joadie. She must be crazy about Joadie; after all, she'd killed for him, and greater love hath no man than a woman who'd kill for him. What the hell did Joadie have to arouse such powerful feelings in Lily? And she'd have to know a hell of a lot about him. How to make her talk? Threaten to skin her? She was a hard lady; wouldn't scare easy. Knock her around a bit? Even though she deserved it, he didn't care for the idea. She was a bitch killer, and he should be glad to batter her, squeeze out what she knew, but all he could think of was how horny she made him feel. It's our damned animal nature, he thought.

He remembered the time they had sex, and that it was then she tipped him off, though she may not have wanted to, about Julie; she'd been softened by the sex. He just might repeat that scene; after good sex, many women seemed ready to give you everything.

He walked to the window, looked out, crouched and crawled out the door, holding his gun. There was the Comanche to worry about; he might have caught up and be skulking. Fargo scrutinized the trees, rocks, bushes; it all looked quiet; dead quiet. He went back to the cabin, picked up Red, a big man, but not heavy, put his body out in the bushes. He'd bury him later. He went back to the cabin and studied Lily, still lying there, but she'd moved a bit. His eyes again studied her breasts, pushing out like pears, and he cursed as he felt tingles in his groin. It'd be like screwing a black widow spider, he told himself.

Her eyes opened and she looked at him with animal cunning; she remembered that she'd shot Red and was wondering what he'd do.

He crouched over her, unbuttoned her shirt, and her white breasts jumped out. Now she'd know.

"What the hell do you think . . ." she snarled.

He stared at her. "You accused me of rape. Might as well keep that record straight," he growled. And unbuttoned her pants.

She squirmed, her eyes angry. "You skunk. I didn't think you that low."

"It is low to do this to a woman who tried to get me lynched. But I'm a forgiving man." He pulled her pants down, revealing her white rounded belly, the short-haired bush and the teasing red lips between her thighs.

She tried to wriggle away, but he held her, and

106

she realized it'd be useless to struggle. "Joadie will kill you for this," she said.

He glowered. "I'm looking forward to meeting Joadie." He put his hand over her pink-nippled breast, it was silky; he felt tightening in his groin.

"Of course, it's ridiculous to think you can rape a saloon girl," he said as he unbuttoned his jeans and brought out his swollen excitement.

She looked at it and her eyes went round as marbles; she shivered a bit.

He spread her legs, brought himself to the scarlet crease, put his tip to it, then plunged all the way.

She was warm and juicy; her body was ready. There was a long pause, while she felt his bigness, then she sighed, "Fargo, you bastard," and put her arms around him.

He felt the pleasure of her, but tried to keep in mind that she was a bitch killer who had tried to get him lynched and did other rotten things. It mixed anger with desire, and he began to plunge hard, rubbing her breasts, and as time went on he picked up the pace, feeling fury and desire, turning his body into a battering ram, coming almost out and thrusting in all the way. She screeched a bit, panted, moaned. She arched her body, and her arms clutched him as he speared her to the bed. And, as happened once before in Dakota, what he thought would be punishment for a woman turned out to be ecstasy. He felt himself climbing to the pitch of tension, swelling enormously, pausing on the peak for a moment, then firing.

It was easy next morning to follow Joadie's prints; they were one-day old and moved at an easy pace. Julie rode behind, which, Fargo realized, tended to slow Joadie down. She had to believe that Fargo, if he survived all the mayhem thrown at him along the route by Joadie, Red and the Comanches, would still be hot on their trail. She probably did what she could to obstruct Joadie's pace.

Where was Joadie taking her, he wondered? And why? Of course, Julie was a beautiful woman and a natural prize in a territory where even a plain woman was desirable. Why would he hang on to Julie, a woman whose family he'd killed? He'd have to know that, given a chance, she'd shoot him like a rattler. He probably held the reins of her horse and had her hands tied. She'd be a wildcat otherwise.

He glanced at Lily riding behind him. No rope on her wrists and riding free. She knew it'd be useless to try to escape. But Lily was not interested in escape; she liked the idea that Fargo, with his trailsmanship, was taking her directly to Joadie. She wanted nothing better. He had gone over her carefully, found no concealed weapons. The only weapon left was her tongue, and she didn't hesitate to use it, telling him that once they caught up, Joadie would make mincemeat of him.

They went through lush country, gentle sloping hills, a meadowland of yellow daffodils, beds of purple violets, a tract of tall pines. When they came to a stream where Joadie and Julie had camped, Fargo too stopped and brought out jerky, beans and coffee.

As he drank he stared at Lily's pretty face, and in turn she stared back, brazenly. She was all guts, no brains, he decided. Why, for example, with one shot in her pistol, did she kill Red? She could have shot him to wipe out the opposition. He didn't mind in the least, of course, that she had used the bullet to shut Red up, fearful of what he'd reveal.

Almost without trying, she sat seductively, her breasts thrown out, her body curved as if to entice him. She probably sat like that with Red at the campfire; she was a trap for the male.

Her brazen look ticked him off, made him try to figure her out.

"Tell me, Lily, you had one bullet in your pistol. Why'd you hit Red instead of me?"

"Uh, yes, I shoulda shot you," she said viciously.

He grinned. "You just lost your head, was that it? Had to shut Red up? A bit foolish, now that you think of it. Right?"

Her eyes were cunning and she shrugged. "Think that if you want."

The tone of her voice, the gleam in her eye jolted him. Maybe she did know what she was doing? There had been fear and anger in her voice when she argued with Red. Why had she feared him? If she feared him, she might want him dead.

"So you thought it was the right move to put Red on ice, did you? I thought he was your dear friend."

Her face flashed anger. "He was too dear."

Suddenly it hit him. "Aha, you had a tumble with Red, was that it?"

She glared. "Go to hell, Fargo."

That *was* it! She'd tumbled Red on the trail, and it meant that Red had power over her, for if he ever dropped a hint to Joadie that she'd put out for him on the trail, there'd be hell to pay. She was all wrapped up in Joadie, but somehow she'd tumbled Red. How much easier to tell Joadie that she had to shoot Red to stop him because he wanted to spill his guts. Fargo finished his coffee. Perhaps, he thought, she had more brains than he gave her credit for.

"So you got friendly one lonely night on the trail—was that what happened, Lily?"

She glared at him viciously. "You raped me, Fargo. When Joadie hears about it, what do you suppose he's going to do?"

Fargo grinned. "I suppose he'll defend your honor. And I'd like nothing better. But Joadie doesn't look to me like a red-blooded man who'd stand and shoot it out. If he was, he wouldn't be running."

"He's not running," she said contemptuously.

She seemed wrapped up in her picture of Joadie as a red-blooded, two-fisted man; if he blasted that a bit, she might let something slip.

"Well, Lily, all I've seen is his backside, all the way from Pottsville. Looks like and smells like a man on the run."

She sneered. "He's going somewhere, you fool, not running from you."

He grabbed her arms, twisted them behind her.

"You bastard," she hissed, "let me go. Joadie will—"

"Screw Joadie. I want the truth out of you. I'll break your arms if you don't talk." He twisted a bit more.

She gasped. "Fargo—he never told me why—just that he had to go to Waco. With Julie."

Fargo softened his grip. "Why with Julie? Why is he taking her? What's in Waco?"

"He never told me. Just to trust him, that he wouldn't touch a hair on her head, that she meant nothing to him, that I was his woman."

Fargo's instinct was to believe her, and turning away, he caught movement high on the slope. The Comanche, damn him, seemed always to be around in moments of emotion, as if they were strategic times to try for a move.

Fargo stood and stared at the crag to telegraph

110

that he knew the Comanche was there. It was then the redskin materialized, as if from the boulder; he stood there showing his great-muscled body in its breechclout silhouetted against the sky. He stood still as a statue, as if to let Fargo know that he was not safe, that he'd never be safe as long as the Comanche stayed on his trail.

Fargo looked at him hard. He had to remember this brave had saved his life back in Lemon Creek. He had a thick chest, rippling gut muscles, powerful legs. He stood there calmly, as if daring Fargo to pull his rifle. Then he moved slightly and seemed to melt into the boulder.

Fargo pulled a cheroot and lit it. No doubt about it, the Comanche had showed himself just to remind Fargo that he was waiting for the moment to kill, for the moment of revenge.

A shame, Fargo thought, that he'd be forced to fight the Comanche; it was kill or be killed. Though the Indian had saved him from a lynching, the redskin would track him until either one or the other was destroyed.

It took another day and a half, pushing hard, to pick up fresh prints. After close ground scrutiny, Fargo guessed that Julie and Joadie had passed this spot within two hours. At a small stream he let the horses drink. "I think, Lily, you'll soon be feasting your eyes on your honeyboy," he said grimly.

Lily's voice was calm. "I look forward to it." Her sly smile seemed to say that, for Fargo, the meeting would be most unfortunate.

He stroked the pinto's flanks. "Tell me, Lily, what's Joadie got that makes you so mad about him, willing to do such great things for him? Must be a powerhouse in bed."

She smiled broadly. "Oh, he's that. He's a smart man, Fargo. I warned you. You won't beat a man like Joadie Smith."

He nodded. "I'll give it a try."

She had a hell of a lot of confidence in that killer bastard.

He studied the trail ahead and the land behind. It was lush, thick with trees, foliage, shrubs. In front of him the killer Joadie with Julie, behind him a deadly Comanche. What were his choices? Should he try to take the Comanche out first? Could he concentrate on Joadie if part of his mind worried about the Comanche? And this redskin would be one tough nut: he had patience, made no reckless moves, stuck with the trail. He could strike anytime; it was dangerous to ignore him. And what about Julie? Now that Joadie was in range of his gun, he might be able to cut her loose from the man who killed her family. It had to be hell to Julie to be forced to travel with him, to be in his power.

Not the Comanche, not yet, but Joadie Smith must be the target. And from the prints he couldn't be far off. "Let's go," he said roughly to Lily and moved the pinto out at a quick pace.

The sun turned yellow, primrose and orange as it began to sink. As Fargo rode he thought of Joadie. He was a lethal man, a killer, leader of a bunch of killers. How would such a man treat Julie? He had told Lily that he wouldn't hurt Julie. Was it true? What kind of a man was he? Did he, a killer, really care for Lily? Or did she just play with dreams.

Now they were in green country, tall pines, tall shrubs, tall grass. The prints were fresh, and Fargo's nerves began to tingle. He felt on the edge of something. He gazed behind, then in front. He pulled his reins, then his gun, turned to Lily. His voice was hard. "I'm putting a rope on you and a gag. To keep you quiet. I'll be back soon. Don't give me trouble, or you'll be sorry."

Her mouth tightened, but she reined up and swung off her horse. It took just minutes to rope and gag her.

Fargo trotted the pinto awhile longer, then tethered it and moved quietly forward on the crouch. Something was ahead, right on the trail. Noiselessly, he approached it, his eyes scanning every shrub, tree, rock. There, perched against a fallen log, was a woman—Julie! Her hands and legs were tied, a gag around her mouth. His skin crawled; what the hell was the meaning of this?

She looked at him, then away, her eyes were wild: was she in pain? He wanted to run and unloosen the ropes, but paused to study the terrain again. Could be bait. Joadie might be lurking in the shrubs, waiting to blast him the moment he reached her.

He made a circle, worked his way north of the log, where the thickets could hide a man. The south had only short grass. He heard nothing, saw nothing.

His mind raced: why had Joadie dumped her? Fear? Did he think he'd never escape the relentless tracker behind him? That he might have a chance alone? There could be no other reason. No sign of Joadie anywhere—the yellowbelly just dumped her and made his run. Didn't matter, he'd still hunt him down like a mad dog. Poor Julie, she had to be in pain—that wild look in her eyes, it grabbed him— her ropes were too tight, or the gag was suffocating.

He went to her quickly, cut the ropes, pulled off the gag.

"Are you hurt, Julie? What's the matter?" he asked with concern.

The voice behind him was harsh, mocking. "It's me that's the matter, Fargo. Don't move or you're dead."

Fargo was electrified: it was impossible for *anyone* to be behind him. But the voice went on. "Now pull your gun and be very careful. I want you dead, mister, and don't need much excuse."

His hand felt numb as he pulled his gun.

"Right, now drop the gun right behind you."

Fargo's mind raced; he'd been outwitted, but how? How did that bastard get behind him? There was no way. A wave of fury and frustration rushed over him. He had missed this slimy polecat, the worst of them all. A hand behind him picked up the gun. Then he heard the soft step, and a big man, almost as tall as himself, moved in front of him, brushing dirt from his hair and his clothes, his face. A high-cheeked, broad-boned face with dead black eyes, a gash of a mouth, and the face was still grimed with dirt. Dirt! He'd come out of the earth; Fargo cursed inwardly. He'd overlooked one trick, but it was not the kind used by a white man; a Comanche, yes: to put out bait that lured the hunter to stop, then to come out of the ground for attack!

Fargo took a slow look behind him at the earth; Joadie had cut into the grass with his shovel edge, taking out enough grass blocks to fit the size of his body, stacked them near him, then covered himself, leaving the earth undisturbed. Fargo cursed again; he would have noticed bent grass, something, if he had not been caught off guard by the sight of Julie in pain. But Julie had not been in pain; she'd been trying to throw a signal with her eyes, urging him to look behind. Well, there it was. The killer Joadie had a gun on him and prospects looked bleak as hell.

114

Joadie brushed the dirt from his face and clothing.

"Gotta hand it to you, Joadie—that was the slickest trick I've ever seen."

Joadie's face was cold. "Don't bullshit me, Fargo. You're a dead man." He glanced at Julie. "Don't make one wrong move, miss, or I'll massacre both of you."

He brushed more dirt from his hair, stared hard at Fargo. "You gave me a helluva lot of trouble, mister. I never thought you'd get this far." He sauntered to a rock half sunk in the earth, sat on it, studied Fargo, then said, "I hafta believe they're all dead." His voice was toneless. "Bowie, Red, Burt, Scotty, Tom." He paused and his eyes glittered. "Lily."

A tingle went through Fargo. "Lily's not dead." The sonofabitch *did* care about Lily—could he use Lily as a stall?

Joadie's mouth twisted. "You're lying."

"I don't shoot women," Fargo said.

Joadie's nostrils widened, the only glimpse of emotion. His eyes had a dead look. "Where is she?"

"I know where she is."

Joadie stood, walked to Fargo, put the gun to his forehead. The gun cocked. "You got one minute before I spill your brains."

"Kill me and you'll never know."

There was a horrible second when the light in Joadie's eyes glared madly and Fargo thought it was all finished. Then Joadie struggled, got control. He stepped back, shifted his gun to his left hand and swung with his right. It was a stinging blow against the jaw and Fargo was jolted.

"Where is she, mister?"

Fargo rubbed his jaw. "If I tell you, you'll shoot, right?"

Again Joadie swung and the blood spurted in Fargo's mouth. The sonofabitch had a fist like a stone. Fargo stared into the dead eyes. He spit blood. "You got a good punch, Joadie. But it's a waste of time. I'll bring you to her."

Joadie glared at him without expression, then stepped back. "I'm going to shoot parts of you away, mister, until you talk."

Julie, who'd been watching, her hand on her breast, cried, "Tell him, for God's sake, Fargo."

Joadie looked at her and his smile was hideous. "Yeah, Fargo. The lady don't want you in pieces. She doesn't like the sight of blood. But you're going to be one bloody mess before I'm through. A bullet for every man you killed—Bowie, Red and the rest."

Fargo shrugged. "You might as well shoot. Because I'll never talk. The only deal is that I take you there."

Joadie studied the ice-blue eyes and something convinced him that this big lean man would do as he said, take the bullets and die with his mouth shut. Well, he didn't have to kill him now, though he felt Fargo was the most dangerous man he'd ever tangled with. But if he kept the gun on him all the time, stayed away from those massive fists, it'd be all right. When they reached Lily, there'd be time to avenge Red and Bowie and shoot this bastard to pieces.

"All right," he said. "We'll get the horses. Now you just walk up the trail east, and you too, honeygirl. Just stay out in front of me. Remember I'm behind you—and I'd just as soon knock off both of you and go my ways. Just don't tempt me."

Julie, walking alongside Fargo, spoke in a low tone. "I tried to warn you with my eyes."

116

Fargo glanced at her, the green eyes, clouded now in the lovely face. "Did he hurt you?"

Her lips were tight. "No, always threatened to if I tried something. He's going somewhere, and taking me along."

Fargo ground his teeth. "I underestimated him. Didn't think he'd have the brains to dig a hole."

"What now?"

"We'll have to see. Once he gets Lily, he won't have any use for me. He's smart enough to kill then."

"Don't bring him to her," she said.

"Can't stall indefinitely." He was silent. "There's a Comanche out there."

She stared. "Because of Red Wolf!"

He nodded. "He saved me from a lynch party. Wants me for himself. I'm hoping to bring Joadie into his range."

Joadie's voice came at them harshly. "What are you two gabbing about? Thinking up a scheme? Don't waste your breath. Once we get on those horses, Fargo, you got twenty minutes. Then you're dead if we don't reach Lily. You'll die slow, with six bullets in you."

There was a flat finality to his voice and Fargo didn't doubt him for a moment. He had killed a woman and a small boy, without raising an eyebrow, and probably left a trail of corpses wherever he'd been.

They came on two horses tethered to a tree branch, Julie's spirited black and a gray gelding.

Joadie never took his eyes off Fargo, holding his gun always ready. He was a tough cookie, Fargo thought, remembering that Lily once said he was smart as a fox.

They rode west, Fargo in front, Julie behind and

Joadie bringing up the rear. Fargo's mind, whipped by the realization that a clever, ruthless killer had him on the shooting end of a six-gun, raced around in search of an out. The Comanche was only a slight possibility: he would have to be there, be ready to act and be willing to act. The odds on that were lousy. Lily? what would happen then? He had kept her alive; perhaps she might put in a word for him. But she'd rather have him dead, since he too knew of her tumble with Red. A thought struck him and he grinned.

He slowed his pinto, so that he was riding just in front of Joadie's gelding.

"I'd like to tell you something about Lily," he said.

The black eyes narrowed. "Go ahead."

"You think that I killed Red, don't you? Well, Lily did."

After a long long silence, during which his hands gripped hard at the reins, Joadie said, "If you're lying, it will be even worse for you, mister. I'll stake you out in the sun for the red ants."

Fargo just smiled casually. "She killed him, she says, to shut him up. And that's true. Because she didn't want what happened"—Fargo paused significantly—"to get back to you."

Joadie's jaw hardened, but he said nothing, then turned to stare at Fargo. Still he said nothing, just motioned for Fargo to return to his former position.

As Fargo moved forward he smiled grimly: he'd given Joadie a lot to think about, and Joadie wasn't going to throw lead until he dug out what really happened. It'd be easy to feel queasy about a woman like Lily, and maybe his hint could feed Joadie's own suspicions. No need to spell out anything.

As they pounded near the terrain where he'd

tied up Lily, Fargo felt a flicker of anxiety. Anything might have happened. The Comanche might have picked her up and played a couple of games with a paleface before he closed in on his real quarry. A hungry animal might have taken a bite out of her. His fears were unfounded, for there she sat against the tree, her hands tied, the gag in her mouth.

At the sight of Joadie, Lily's eyes lit up as with a hundred candles. Even through the gag she called his name as if it was the sweetest sound in the language, and Fargo had to believe that in spite of her profession as a saloon girl, she was mad about Joadie.

He watched Joadie as he swung off his horse, cut her ropes, took the gag from her mouth and stuck Fargo's gun in her belt.

"Off the horses," Joadie ordered, his gun ready, never taking his eyes from Fargo.

No question about it, Fargo thought, Joadie was smart as a fox and a hell of a survivor. Look at the way he buried himself in the earth. That was a masterstroke. Maybe he had to respect the man who plowed through Bowie, Red and Burt. Maybe too he felt threatened every moment he let this tracker live. This man had tracked him like a famished wolf. But Joadie had been touched in a crucial spot—Lily. He was crazy about her and jealous as a tiger. Sure, he had used Lily to stall the big, dangerous Fargo, but her feelings were not involved, so that was all right. But Joadie suffocated with rage and jealousy at the thought that she had tumbled Red. Joadie had to thrash out the truth before he could do anything.

Somehow Fargo could read Joadie's mind, and he

understood his life wasn't worth two pins to this man who, at any moment, could kill viciously.

Fargo, watching the dark brooding eyes in Joadie's face, felt that the poison he'd planted in Joadie's mind had worked. A man in a jealous rage, even one like Joadie, might lose his concentration and that's what he had to wait for—and there couldn't be much time. This killer couldn't feel right until he'd killed the thing that threatened him; it was how he stayed alive, and he knew that Fargo alive was a deadly threat.

Lily rushed to Joadie, threw her body against his, her arms tight about him. Then she kissed his face, over and over. Joadie accepted it all, just kept his eyes on Fargo, his gun ready.

Julie's horse had gone off to graze at some rich grass patch twenty yards away, and Fargo sat on the ground, his hands drooping over his lap. He looked as impotent as a man could without a gun.

Lily was gushing. "I told him he could never beat you, I told him you were smarter than him. I told him he'd pay for the misery he'd done."

"What misery, Lily?" His eyes were on Fargo.

She stared. "Why, all the misery. He's killed Bowie, Burt, Scotty, Tom. And dragged me through hell on this trail. If you hadn't been at the end of his trail, I couldn'ta done it."

"What happened to Red, Lily?" Joadie's voice was toneless.

Her eyes widened, and it finally occurred to her that something in his attitude was different. She shot a venomous look at Fargo, then said, "Red's dead, Joadie. I'm sorry."

There was a long pause. "How'd it happen, Lily?" He still watched Fargo, and his voice had a deadness to it.

"How? I shot him." Her voice quavered. "I shot him because Fargo was squeezing his guts, trying to make him talk."

"Talk about what, Lily?"

She pulled back and put her hands on her hips. "What is it, Joadie? What's the matter?"

"Talk about what, Lily?" the toneless voice repeated.

Her hand went to her neck and stroked it. "He wanted to know who hired you men to do that job on the Davis family. Wanted to know all about Burt and the boys, where they came from. And Red was talking."

For one moment the dead eyes moved from Fargo to her. "But Red didn't know anything, Lily."

She bit her lip, just looked at him.

"He didn't *know* anything," Joadie repeated, not looking at her, only at Fargo.

There was a heavy silence. Fargo just sat, his hands between his knees; Julie watched with tight lips, leaning against a tree trunk.

"Why'd you shoot him, Lily?"

Her voice had a desperate edge. "I just told you. I thought he was going to spill his guts."

"But you *knew* he didn't know anything, Lily."

Again that heavy silence. Julie was watching, fascinated, sensing the powerful jealousy churning in the big man with the gun.

Suddenly Lily pointed to Fargo, and her voice rasped with suppressed hysteria. "You been listening to that liar, haven't you?"

He spoke slowly. "Fargo said that you shot Red to shut him up."

"That's right—that's what I did."

"Not because he had anything to say—but be-

121

cause you acted like a whore." His eyes glittered
wildly.

She gasped. "That's a filthy lie. He just said it to
get you mad."

"You always wanted Red, didn't you, Lily?
Always."

Her face was distorted. "You're crazy. Don't you
see, it's Fargo, he's the one. If you want the truth—it
was him, Fargo, that raped me on the trail. It's
true, he's the one. Shoot him, kill him!"

He glared at her, showing his feelings for the
first time. "You had it with Red finally, didn't
you? You slut. You can't control it. You had it with
Red. Didn't you?"

She put her hand on her heaving breasts. "Don't
you see what he's done?"

"What he's done. It's what you done, you lying
little bitch." He slapped her hard, which jolted
her, threw her back a few steps. He shot a quick
glance at Fargo, then turned to her. "I always knew
you wanted Red. Even from the beginning. Back in
Waco you wanted Red. You just didn't have the
nerve."

She held her face and glared at him. "You're
crazy, Joadie. It was you, always you."

His slitted eyes shone with rage. "The one time,
the only time I left you with Red—because I had to
take out this girl, you had to be the slut again. You
can't help it. With Red."

She looked at him, at the deadly rage in his eyes.

"You fool, you stupid, miserable, jealous fool, don't
you see what he's done?" She looked around wildly,
then, as if overpowered by her fury, she pulled the
gun from her belt, pointed it at Fargo to shoot, and
Joadie, his eyes almost starting from his head, swung
his gun to her. The bullet hit her heart, and she

122

staggered back two steps, her eyes on Joadie in amazement, and she fell down, never taking her eyes from him, her hand going to her breast, the blood pouring out.

"Why—Joadie?"

His mouth was grim. "Because you just proved it. Tried to shut up Fargo. Like you did Red. To shut them up."

Then she said, "Joadie, there never was anyone but you."

Joadie stared at her, almost paralyzed by what, in a fit of jealousy, he had done. And Fargo, who'd been waiting for the moment, edged his hand into his boot, slipped the thin-bladed knife from its holster and, in one smooth movement, threw it. It hit the wrist that held the gun, cutting tendons, nerves and arteries, and the gun dropped as Fargo hurtled forward, butting Joadie in the gut, driving him back. He scooped up the gun, held it on Joadie sprawled on the ground, in shock, not from the knife in his wrist but from what he'd done to Lily, what she'd said at the point of death. That she loved only him and that, in dying, she had to be telling the truth. He got up slowly, ignoring Fargo, pulled the knife from his wrist, threw it to the ground, then walked to where Lily lay, her eyes still open, dying.

He sat on the ground, next to her.

"You were the only one," she said.

He gritted his teeth. "You took a goddamned funny way of showing it."

Julie stood three feet from him, holding Lily's gun. But he didn't care, the fire seemed gone out of him. He's a goner, Fargo thought. He watched for a few minutes, whistled for the pinto, and when it came, he took the shovel from the saddle.

He came in front of Joadie. "I've got to move fast.

Don't have much time. And gotta have some answers. Why'd you kill the Davis family?"

Joadie said nothing; he seemed to be far away, somewhere in his thoughts.

"Braddock," he said, and a curious look, almost sly came to his face.

"What?" Fargo scowled.

Joadie looked up. "Hired by a man called Braddock." His voice was flat, low, his dark eyes blurred.

"Who's he?"

"Foreman of the T-Ranch in Waco. He wanted to clean out Davis and his brood."

Fargo scowled. "Why'd he want that?"

Joadie shrugged; his voice was mechanical, flat. "Don't know. Didn't say. Maybe he had a grudge. He's a rotten bastard."

"Then what?"

"I picked up the boys and we did it. For the money."

"How'd Burt and the others get into it?"

"Men from the Talley ranch. Braddock sent them to help, in case I needed it. I told them you were interfering, to get rid of you."

Fargo rubbed his chin. "What about Julie? Why'd you grab her?"

"Braddock wanted her. Wanted us to bring her back. But she wasn't there, nowhere around. Then she obliged by coming after us."

Fargo stared. "What the hell did he want Julie for?"

Joadie shook his head. "Don't know. It was part of the deal. There was extra money if we brought her back."

Fargo stared at him: was he telling the truth? He was a shrewd devil, this Joadie. But if true, then Braddock was the man: it all started with him. In

Waco. Well, they'd close in on Mr. Braddock and squeeze the truth out of him.

What about Joadie? They'd take him into Waco, and if there was law, they'd string him up for what he did to the Davis family.

"Bury her," he said, pointing with his gun to the dead Lily. He turned to look at Julie, who'd been listening, her face a mask. She had Lily's gun. "Watch him while I get your horse. We'll take him to Waco. He'll get justice there."

He went after Julie's horse, which had strayed almost twenty yards for its grazing. He never stopped looking at the slope, just in case the Comanche might reappear. Once he glanced at Julie; she was talking to Joadie as he stood near Lily, holding the shovel.

When Fargo finally got to Julie's horse, gathered the reins, he heard a gunshot and wheeled fast, thinking Joadie had tricked the gun from Julie. But she was standing and he was down. She'd shot him.

He'd gone down on his back, lay still for a minute, then he turned over painfully, began to crawl toward Lily and kept crawling till he reached her. Then he got his head next to hers, lay there, then died.

Fargo came back, his face grim. "What the hell did you do that for? I told you we'd take him in."

"I told him," she said in a low voice, "that he'd killed my father, my mother and my brother. That it was a pity that I could kill him only once." Then the arrow whistled past his head, missing by inches. Fargo's gun barked.

He went up the slope, his eyes shifting to grab movement, but could see nothing; Thick foliage and the tree trunk where the Comanche had fired his arrow from. Moccasin prints, the ground smeared when he'd dropped, then his prints up slope. He'd not been hit; at least there was no sign of blood, just a careful Comanche crawling through grass until he couldn't be seen, then swift running tracks.

Fargo looked down; Julie had dug part of a hole. He grimaced as he started back—a grave for a whore and a killer. In love, how'd you explain that? Love was a mysterious disease if it touched two people like them.

So now Joadie was out, but the hunt was still unfinished. He had believed, way back in Pottsville, that Joadie was the end man, the one who'd know the answers—but behind Joadie was Braddock. Like a puppet show with the devil pulling the strings, you knocked down one puppet, another came up. First Bowie, then Red, then Joadie—all gone down. And was it Braddock who was the devil, who really pulled the strings? If so, why, what grudge could he have against Davis to. wipe out his family? He had to be a deeply evil man because the idea to kill originated in his mind; he had to be the worst of the three. Who was Braddock? What was his connection with the Davis family? Braddock held the key.

Braddock.

A big sickle moon threw soft light and dark shadows on the land. It caught the shelter of pines where they had camped four miles out of Waco. He dug a pit and had a small fire burning; he'd shot a jackrabbit and they broiled it, ate it with beans and it tasted fine. Julie, as she drank coffee, stared at him with cool green eyes.

"Who in hell is this Braddock, Fargo?"

126

He shook his head. "We have to nail him to find out."

Her mouth was hard. "Do you think Joadie was telling the truth?"

"Don't know."

Her mouth was hard. "If it's Braddock, then he's the one we've been hunting all the time. The others just did the dirty work, for money."

He nodded.

Her voice sounded bitter. "What'd he have against us? I never heard his name in the house. Never. Why would he do it?"

Fargo lifted his coffee cup; the aroma was bracing. How could he answer? A man did many things in his life, and sometimes he did the wrong thing. Julie's father must have had an unsettled score with Braddock, who finally decided to settle it. Julie, on that day, happened to be elsewhere. Joadie said there'd be a bonus for bringing her back. Why? Well, if you hunted the father and violated the daughter, you got a good piece of revenge, didn't you? But it would have to be a real hard grievance. Could that be the reason he wanted Julie?

As foreman of a ranch, Braddock would be a power—it meant they'd have to be plenty careful, that it could be dangerous in Waco.

"What do you think, Fargo?" she pressed him.

"The only way this makes sense to me is that Braddock and your father had a bad old score between them."

She brooded. "And now I have a score to settle with him." Her voice went intense. "Why, if he had a score to settle, didn't he face Father like a man? Why'd he shoot an innocent boy and my mother? Why?"

Fargo's jaw hardened. It was like that in this

127

world, evil men punishing the innocent. He'd seen it happen again and again. It was a mystery he couldn't explain. All he could do was try and punish such men, if chance brought them into the range of his gun. His own family had been destroyed, and they were innocent, and the rage against the killers burned in him always. Each man that he had destroyed for Julie—Bowie, Red, Joadie—for the moment reduced the rage that seethed in him. He was fated to live with this rage until he wiped out the cruel killers or was himself wiped out. That's why he went through the territory like a living gun.

"Something of a hyena, this Braddock," he said grimly. He glanced up at the sickle moon, sailing in its ocean of blue, the big stars glittering, swinging in an eternal trail, uncaring about the misery and comedy played out on the earth. There are no answers, he thought, only questions.

Later, in the quiet of the night as he lay on his bedroll, he heard a movement; it was Julie. She wore a thin chemise that showed the swelling rise of her breasts and rounding of her hips. It jolted him because until now, she'd been very modest in how she appeared before him.

"Fargo, are you awake?"

He raised on one elbow. "What is it?"

"I'm not sleepy. Can we talk just a bit?"

He smiled. "Sure."

She sat on the grass, leaned back on her hands, a movement that pushed her breasts forward. He sighed, not a good idea for her to be that close, especially as he'd worked hard to stay in control. He hated fighting temptation.

"I've been thinking about Joadie," she said.

"What about him?" he asked, surprised.

"I shot him, yes, in cold blood, and he deserved

128

it. While I was riding with him, and you were tracking us, I thought of him as an animal, not human. I kept looking for a chance to blast his rotten guts."

Fargo listened; her face in the pale moonlight was beautiful.

"I thought him an animal," she said. "Then, when he came together with Lily, that strange thing happened."

Fargo remembered.

She patted her long hair, which gleamed in the moonlight.

"Imagine it, a dog like him. He killed Lily because she'd been disloyal to him—with Red. Because of jealousy. But she loved him. Then, when he was dying, he crawled to get to her. To be near her when he died."

Her voice quavered. "Didn't think he could feel at all. A man who killed people like they were bugs. So, tell me, Fargo, how could he be a killer and a lover?"

Fargo took a deep breath and looked at the pines shrouded in darkness and mystery. "He killed her because of jealousy, not love. Does anyone pull a trigger on what he loves? That's not how I see it."

She smiled. "Fargo, you are something. Tell me, why haven't you flirted with me? I feel somewhat insulted."

He grinned. "Don't think it hasn't occurred to me, plenty. You're one beautiful woman. But I felt your grief. About your family."

She nodded. "You're one understanding brute, Fargo. For a long time I could think of nothing but how to destroy those men. We've done that. There's still Braddock, yes. But it's not been easy riding with a man like you, and forced to behave modestly."

His grin broadened. "There's no reason to be modest now. Is there?"

She smiled. "I can't think of one."

"Then come here," he said.

She came close and he could smell her femaleness. He could see in the moonlight the rise and fall of her breasts, the gleam in the green depths of her eyes.

He kissed her and her lips were soft, full and tasted fresh as a flower petal. He put his arms around her slender waist and held her tightly. He could feel the quick throb of her heart against his chest. He kissed her again, a long kiss, and felt desire scorch his loins. He pulled at her chemise, revealing her breasts. They were rounded, full, and the pink tips, fired by passion, thrust out. He stroked her breast, the fine silk of it, touched the nipple with his fingertip, then put his mouth to it. His hands stroked the curve of her back, her waist, her rounded firm buttocks. Her breathing had quickened; he pulled at her chemise, at her underpants, and she stood there nude, her body like a nymph's, waiting for love. He stripped off his undershirt and stepped out of his shorts. The sight of his inflamed flesh seemed to magnetize her. He took her hand and put it to him. Her body trembled, she seemed overpowered by her feelings. He brought her gently to the bedroll and she lay there, as if in a trance, waiting. His hand moved between her thighs into the velvet warmth; the juices of passion flowed. He touched the spot and she quivered; he stroked her like this, then brought his flesh between her thighs and slipped in a bit at a time; she was amazingly tight. He pushed gently, feeling her flesh surround his fullness. He felt great ripples of pleasure. Slowly, persistently, he pushed until he was entirely engulfed. There was an extraordinary newness in his feelings, as if he was having a woman for the first time. It was almost an ecstatic feeling. He looked down; her eyes were closed, as in a dream, and the pleasure in her face was inescapably clear.

He began to move, keeping his flesh pressed high against her, where the pleasure for her was greatest. He kept his body moving in strong rhythms, while he held her breasts, her hips, her buttocks. Her body felt like satin to his touch. Now the tension began to climb and his thrusts became stronger, and each thrust into her body seemed to intensify his pleasure. His grip on her buttocks went fierce; he clenched, tensed and thrust for the last time as he felt his mind and body empty in a poignant gush of pleasure. Her body heaved, twisted, and she seemed to tighten into a coil of nerves, then suddenly broke free. And a long, long sigh came from her pressed lips.

She lay for a few minutes, staring up at the stars, as if she were dreaming awake. Then she lifted her body, took his face in her hands and kissed him.

"I didn't know," she whispered, "that anything could be like that, Fargo."

7

They were about two miles out of Waco on a wide
trail when he heard the crack of a whip behind
him, and yippie-ai-a of a cowboy. A buggy came
trundling up fast, with a driver and a woman, and,
behind them, five cowboys on spirited horses.

The driver, a powerful, thick-necked, broad-
cheeked man, played the whip lightly on the flanks
of the two beautiful bays, and they dashed so fast
that Fargo and Julie were forced to the side of the
road.

It was bad driving manners, arrogance even, and
Fargo stared hard-eyed at the driver. He wore a
brown Stetson, a tan vest with a gold chain, and his
light blue eyes scanned Fargo and Julie indiffer-
ently as he swept past. Fargo, irritated, scarcely
glanced at the woman whose face was not visible
behind the bonnet. She, however, glanced at them.

The four cowboys were more enthusiastic in the
way they looked at Julie, and one let out an appre-
ciative yell as he went past, sweeping off his hat
gallantly. Julie, though also annoyed at the arrogance
of the driver, couldn't help smile at the cowboy.

"Nice fella, that driver," Fargo said sarcastically
as they watched the buggy speed round a turn in
the trail.

It was two hours to sundown.

Waco was a thriving town, its main street throbbing with life—cowboys and wranglers, farmers and cattlemen gossiping on porches and in the streets, wagons loading, buggies riding through. The shops and houses were sturdy, two-storied, with fresh coats of white paint. This was mostly cattle country, and prosperous.

Fargo reserved two rooms at the Jones Hotel, a clean, cheerful place, then stopped with Julie at Harding's Steak House, a spacious restaurant with cloths on the table.

Harding, a ruddy smiling man with straw-colored hair, came to take their order.

"Two broiled steaks, smothered in onions, home fries, corn on the cob and hot buttered biscuits." Fargo smiled in anticipation of a real meal instead of trail food.

Harding looked pleased. "Mister, we like to serve hungry folks coming into town." He called a slender young Mexican. "Gomez, take this order, tell cook to make it extra special." He turned to Fargo. "Where you folks from, if I'm not too nosy?" His tone was genial.

"West Texas." Fargo on principle rarely volunteered such information.

"Well, folks, you'll like Waco. It's big, getting bigger. Finest cattle country in the state. Everything's great in Waco."

Fargo grinned. "Let's see how great the steaks are, Harding."

When Gomez brought out the sirloins, Fargo's eyes were saucer-wide. They were giant slabs of meat, brown and juicy. He did a man's job on his, and even Julie was astonished at the way he demolished it. She could manage only half her portion.

When Harding came back, he grinned. "We also have some delicious pecan pie."

"Bring it on, two cuts for me," said Fargo, "and some coffee."

Fargo glowed after he finished the pie, so that when Harding came back the third time, he said, "If things in Waco are as great as the food, you've got a helluva town, mister." He paused. "Tell me, do you know Braddock?"

"Sure I know Braddock. Everyone knows him. Good man to know."

"Why's that?"

Harding shrugged. "A big man. Runs the Big T, the Talley ranch, the biggest and richest land in the territory. Doesn't hurt to be on the right side of him."

"Where can I find him?"

"Well, nights he comes to Murphy's, the saloon, to drink a few beers and play poker. Likes that."

Fargo rubbed his chin. "So he works for Talley? And who's Talley?"

Harding shook his head. "You're a stranger all right. Talley is dead. It's Mrs. Talley's place now. Twenty thousand head of cattle, and twenty miles of the richest land in the county. A lot of ranch to run, and she needed help. She put Braddock right alongside her. He runs the ranch with a strong hand. It's common talk that he's angling to get even closer to the Widow Talley. A handsome woman. That's where he wants to be, top man of the T ranch. An ambitious man, Braddock."

Fargo stood up and rubbed his stomach. "My gut is sure grateful, Harding. Best food we've had in a month of Sundays."

*   *   *

Fargo walked into Murphy's. It was one of those big saloons that could take in fifty men. Three bartenders shoveled out beer and whiskey, and a "bouncer" with a shotgun sat on a raised chair. Men played poker on five gambling tables. A stairway in the back led to the second floor, where saloon ladies entertained the more zealous customers.

Fargo ordered whiskey from a blue-eyed barman with a green bow tie and a .44 Colt in his holster.

"New in town, mister?"

"Yeah, Fargo's the name."

"Welcome, Mr. Fargo. You look like the kinda man who'd like it. Lots of work and good money. Interested?"

Fargo shrugged. "If you are, just talk to that big man at the end table, Braddock. He'll give you a fair shake. But see him after the game. Hates to be interrupted."

Fargo tossed off his drink, and when the barman refilled it, he paid and took it with him to Braddock's game table. He recognized Braddock as the driver who had hogged the trail with his buggy earlier in the day. Fargo mixed with the men watching the game, taking a position where he could see Braddock. A muscular man with hefty shoulders, a thick neck and thick chest. He had a broad-cheeked face with intense blue eyes that tended to stare, and while he seemed to be a hardhead, he also seemed to laugh a lot and enjoy a good time. He was winning and it put him in good humor. Fargo studied his playing and noted his willingness to bluff big.

After winning a sizable pot, Braddock laughed, and as he raked in the money he glanced at the onlookers, wanting appreciation of his clever playing.

When he looked at Fargo, his eyes stayed on him as if trying to put him into a pigeonhole, but he couldn't and it made him frown. But he nodded, and Fargo nodded too, but his eyes were hard. Braddock sensed the challenge and his jaw tightened.

"What's the name, stranger?"

"Fargo, Skye Fargo."

The name didn't register, but the feelings he sensed in Fargo did, and he picked up the gauntlet. "Care to sit in, Fargo?" He smiled insolently. "You look like you can afford to lose money."

The men standing nearby laughed. They stopped when Fargo looked at them. "I'll be glad to play, Braddock. But I don't count on losing."

Braddock grinned. "Just try counting your money after the game. Make room for Mr. Fargo," he said, glancing at the men, and they grinned, taking the cue from him that this stranger should get a riding.

They began to play and the pots shifted around, going most often to the man on Fargo's right, a gray, stooped man named Rufus.

As the game went on, Braddock, in the guise of friendliness, tried to get a fix on the stranger sitting opposite him. "Where you from, Fargo?"

"Lotta places, Braddock. Came through the Dakota territory and west Texas."

"That right? What's your work?"

"Trailsman."

The blue eyes stared. "Always on the move? Ever think of settling in one place?"

"Not often."

Braddock still couldn't make up his mind whether Fargo was for or against him, and after the next pot had been won, he said, "It's a pity you won't settle. You look like the kinda man we'd like on the Talley ranch. We need good men and the money's good. It's a growing country."

"If the Comanches let it grow," Fargo said.

"We'll have the redskins licked. Either wipe them out or put them on reservations."

They played another uneventful pot. Braddock seemed more interested in probing Fargo. "Where'd you come through, Fargo?"

"I started out in Eagle Butte," Fargo said, the town near Julie's home.

The name seemed to get no reaction from Braddock. He looked at his cards, stared hard, tightened his lips, then said, "Trailsman, huh. Trailing anyone just now, Fargo, or just enjoying the trail scenery?"

The men smiled; they had to enjoy the boss's humor, Fargo realized. He looked at his cards. Two tens, a queen, a five and a two. "Well," he drawled, "I was trailing someone—you might know him."

"Who would that be?"

"A man called Joadie Smith." Fargo looked hard at Braddock. He wondered if the blue of those eyes darkened, but they never wavered, looked straight back at him.

"Yeah, I know Joadie. Why were you trailing him?"

"He did some shooting back in Eagle Butte. Killed a family."

Braddock's eyes narrowed, and a flurry of feelings seemed to rush through them, but his face never changed its expression. Then he looked at his men standing around. "Joadie Smith," he said slowly, "was a rotton lowdown thief, a liar, a hyena of a man. I ran him out of the ranch myself." He shook his head. "Yeah, I know Joadie all right."

There was heavy silence, the men looking at Braddock, then at Fargo.

"So what happened to Joadie?"

"What do you mean?" Fargo asked.

137

Braddock's face was grim. "You were trailing him, you said. Where is he now?"

"Pushing daisies," Fargo said.

There was foot scuffling among the men, and Braddock's eyes narrowed. He spoke slowly. "Joadie was a fast gun and smart as a wolf. If you beat Joadie in a fair fight, then, Mr. Fargo, you got to be a damned good gun. How many cards?"

"Two," said Fargo.

The other players each took three, Braddock took one. He's going to bluff, Fargo told himself.

"So what brought you to Waco, Fargo?" Braddock asked, looking at his draw. His face was impassive.

"Something Joadie said."

"What'd he say?"

Fargo shuffled his five cards, not looking at his draw yet. "He said somebody hired him to do that job, kill off the Davis family and rob the place."

Braddock looked pained. "So that's what he did?" He shook his head. "A hyena of a man, I told you. If he did what you said, we'd take care of him here, right, men?"

The men grunted agreement. They were big, beefy men, and looked like they were capable of a lot of damage.

Braddock couldn't keep his eyes off Fargo. It was like he wanted to turn Fargo inside out and examine him. "So you came to Waco to get accounts squared—that's interesting. Riding alone, I take it?" A casual remark, but Fargo felt it loaded with dynamite.

It could mean he knew something about Julie or it could be just a wild remark, nothing intended.

Fargo shook his head, noncommittal. "Let's play poker."

Braddock looked at his cards. "Yeah, let's play," he said. "I bet fifty dollars."

The other three players gaped, then threw in their cards.

Fargo too stared at him; the blue eyes were steady as a rock, and he continued to look into them. Braddock had drawn one and would have either two pair, four of a kind or be playing for a flush. But Fargo had picked up something and was ready to back his hunch. Braddock might have a pair, and it could be better than two tens, but Fargo felt that Braddock was ready for the big bluff. At the beginning of the game he'd bragged that he'd empty Fargo's pockets, and he felt belligerent about Fargo, a feeling he'd submerged, but it could now be expressed by cutting Fargo's balls off with a bluff hand.

"Fifty to cover and up you fifty," Fargo said.

That jarred Braddock and he took a careful look at Fargo. He figured the cards; Fargo had drawn two, but that didn't mean anything. Might have three or trying for two pair or bluffing. But Braddock knew that when in doubt his heavy bets always pushed out his opponent; if there was too much to lose, a player, even if he thought he had strong cards, would pull back and drop out.

"Fifty in and up you a hundred." He was confident this would scotch Fargo's nerve.

But Fargo was already betting his hunch and it was based on something he had picked up in Braddock's playing. "A hundred to cover, and up you another hundred."

A gasp came from the onlookers crowded around, many having come from other parts of the saloon.

Braddock's blue eyes stayed rock steady. "A hundred in and up you five hundred."

Fargo had to smile. This tactic was to force the player out by running him out of funds. "I'll see that." Fargo's voice was cool.

"Let's see the color of your money." Braddock's mouth was tight. He was astounded that Fargo had the guts to stick, especially when so much money was involved.

Fargo pulled out a leather pouch, took out several gold pieces. "There it is. Now show yours."

Braddock shook his head in disbelief, pulled out his leather pouch. The steady blue eyes, Fargo noticed, were no longer steady. They moved about, and Fargo felt certain there was no powerhouse hand on that table. Braddock might beat him, but if he did, it wouldn't be by much; he had that feeling in his bones.

Fargo laid out his cards. Two tens, that was it!

A gasp went up from the crowd.

"You sonofabitch," said Braddock.

Fargo's gun was out, a lightning draw that left everyone petrified. "I don't think you meant that, Braddock." Fargo's voice was frosty.

Braddock shook his head. "No, Fargo, I didn't mean it as an insult. I was admiring your nerve. Put your gun up. If you used it, even if you got me, you'd never get out of here alive. I've got twenty men here who'd pay you off."

Fargo nodded pleasantly. "That makes good sense. But I don't allow people to call me names. Now I've paid a lot of money to see your cards. Show 'em."

Braddock with a smile put down his cards. A pair of sixes!

There was a terrific moment of silence, then a spontaneous roar from the onlookers. They'd been thrilled by the nerve of two men betting a fortune on nothing at all, each trying to outnerve the other. It

140

was a spectacular piece of cardplaying that touched the men, because gambling like that revealed character, coolness under fire, the talent for craftiness—qualities that made for survival in a cruel territory where you lived by your wits.

Fargo and Braddock were smiling at each other, and as Fargo reached for the pile of gold pieces on the table, there was spontaneous foot stamping. But Fargo was thinking of how he had outbluffed Braddock; he'd noticed, as a spectator, that when Braddock would bluff big, his eyes would go extra steady, as if he knew a furtive look betrayed a bad conscience; it was an unconscious giveaway, and it gave Fargo the edge.

Braddock put out his hand, and after a moment, Fargo shook it. He didn't know yet if Joadie's story was true or not. It'd take detective work, but till then, perhaps, Braddock should be treated innocent till proved guilty. Moreover, he was in the territory of the enemy; you didn't challenge him there unless you were an eighteen-carat fool.

"I'll give you a chance to even it up another time, Braddock. But I have a friend at the hotel that I gotta look in on."

Braddock also stood. "I'll take you at your word to play again. Not for the money I lost. I like a good game."

Fargo walked back along Main Street toward the hotel in the dark of the night; lamps glowed in the windows. His pouch felt heavy with the pieces of gold and he thought a bit about Braddock. Not an easy man to figure out.

He climbed the stairs of the hotel, tapped lightly on Julie's door. She opened it partly, her gun out.

She let him in, holstered her gun with a smile. "Once kidnapped, twice shy."

He walked to the window and looked out—the stars in the night sky shone like big diamonds, freshly polished. A couple of cowboys feeling their drinks walked unevenly toward their horses, singing a familiar song in an unrecognizable key. A well-behaved respectable town, it seemed.

Fargo turned. "That driver in the buggy, who pushed us off the trail—that was Braddock." He sat on the windowsill and grinned. "Just played poker with him. Taught him a few fine points."

She waited, sitting on the wooden chair, her face impassive.

Fargo pulled his ear. "Not an easy man to figure out, this Braddock. He swears that Joadie is a thief and a liar, that he ran him off the ranch. We were in a card game, and ten of his men must have been watching. Couldn't do much in a place like that. Need to get him alone. He's going to be tough."

Julie turned to the mirror, fluffed her auburn hair, watching Fargo's reflection. "Do you believe Braddock? I mean about Joadie being a liar?"

Fargo thought a moment. "Joadie was a killer, so he sure could be a liar. But it's hard to believe he was lying after he shot Lily. Didn't seem to care anymore. Braddock may be our man. But"—he shook his head—"we have to make sure. We must get him alone and squeeze the truth out of him."

"And the truth, you believe, is he had a blood feud with my father."

"Must have been bad blood between them." Fargo rubbed his chin. "That's if Joadie is to be believed. Braddock may be in the clear. It may be that Joadie got run off by Braddock, hated his guts and blamed him. It may be that Joadie and his boys just happened on your father's place, hit it, found good money and killed to wipe out witnesses. That sort of thing happens a lot."

She took a deep breath. "If that's so, then we've done our job—paid off the men who did the killing. Do you think that's it?"

He considered it: "I don't know. We have to get close to Braddock, somehow."

In his room, ten minutes later, Fargo heard a light step on the stairs and his gun came out. Then a light tap on his door. He slitted the door, his gun ready; he recognized one of the men who stood behind Braddock during the card game.

"Got a minute, Mr. Fargo?" His tone was polite.

Fargo swung the door open.

"My name is Allen. Braddock sent me. He'd like for you and your lady companion to visit the Talley ranch tomorrow." The man had alert brown eyes in a dark-skinned face, a dark beard cut short, close to his face. His brown eyes slipped away from Fargo's eyes, examined the room. The words tumbled out fast. "You made a big impression on Braddock, Mr. Fargo. That game you played. He'd like to offer you the hospitality of the ranch. It's one of the biggest in the Southwest. Hopes you can come out. Promises you and your lady friend a good time."

Fargo grinned. This coyote knew how to pitch a smooth line. "Tell Braddock the lady and me will be glad to come out tomorrow, early afternoon, to look at the famous Talley spread."

Allen's mouth twisted in a humorless grin. "Take the east trail, turn on the second fork. Can't miss it."

*   *   *

Next day after lunch at Harding's, they rode toward the Talley ranch. They were in the middle of a heat wave, and the sun was a yellow blaze in a scalded sky. Fargo felt the sweat stick to his shirt. They stopped at a sparkling stream bordered with hackberry trees to let the horses drink. Julie, with two hands, ran cold water over her face, and Fargo, watching, thought, A beautiful filly.

The sun was still high when they reached the ranch gate; it was made of lacy wrought iron and the name "Talley" was spelled out on top.

Twenty yards beyond the gate, surrounded by manicured grass, a great house, painted brilliant white, bulked against the sky. And nearby, against the trunk of an oak, sat a cowboy, smoking a cheroot: it was Allen. Beyond him, on land that stretched endlessly, Fargo could see great herds of cattle grazing and corrals full of horses.

Allen came up, his dark-skinned face in a pleasant smile. "Braddock said to bring you to the south corral. Some action there."

They rode to a corral from which an occasional shout came up. Cowboys were leaning on a fence watching a rider on a black, powerful stallion, trying to break him. To Fargo, the stallion looked like a demon horse, a killer, like one he'd seen in Dakota who stomped a man to death. This one was big, mean, with great rippling muscles and cruel-looking teeth that he kept baring. He found the rider an unforgivable insult, and he bucked violently, humped and heaved, and the rider, a muscular, redheaded cowboy, sailed fifteen feet into the air. The horse turned to look at the cowboy, then started to trot aggressively toward him, and the cowboy made a frantic run for the fence. It was a comic sight, and the cowboys slapped their thighs with gleeful malice.

"He's a new horse," Allen said, "just came into the corrals."

"That damned stallion is a killer," Fargo muttered as they leaned against the fence. He knew from experience there were stallions, and they were rare, who were killers; tricky, devious—once they cornered a rider they could create mayhem quick as the sting of a rattler.

Fargo could see Braddock at the end of the fence talking hard at a woman with a striking face, wearing tailored riding pants, a fitted blue shirt and fancy boots with spurs. Though she listened to Braddock, her eyes were glued on the stallion, then she shook her head, set her jaw and climbed the fence.

Braddock's big red face creased with worry and he barked at the two men to set up the stallion. It took clever skirmishing for the handlers to get the stallion quiet between them.

The woman approached the horse cool and easy, a quirt in her hand. The stallion eyed her malevolently; his body trembled. Fargo shook his head. "She doesn't know what she's in for, but she's got nerve."

"She's got plenty of nerve," said Allen. "I'm betting on her."

"You can't break a stallion like this," Fargo said.

"She'll do it," said Allen, his tone a bit superior.

The woman had an oval face, white skin, a trim compact figure, and she looked like she could tame anything she wanted. Her spurs tinkled as she walked, and it was clear that she'd come to do rough riding.

It's the stallion, Fargo thought suddenly; she's out to break it though hell freeze over.

"Why's she doing it?" asked Julie with distaste. "What's she trying to prove?"

Fargo smiled. "Maybe that she can do what a man can't. Breaking horses is a man's game."

Julie shot him a mean look. "How do you know, Fargo? She might be a great rider. What counts with a horse is the handling. Not brute strength, not ripping its flanks with your spurs."

A roar broke from the cowboys when the handlers turned the stallion loose and ran to the fence. The horse stood still as a stone statue, then its flanks trembled and it let out a terrified neigh and went up on its back legs, pawing at the sky, trying to slide the hateful burden off its back. The rider instantly struck it a short hard blow with her quirt. The stallion came down, trembled, then began to buck violently, and at each buck the woman struck him with the quirt. The infuriated stallion began to twist and buck, and she hit him again and again; then he sprinted forward, stopped hard and heaved. The woman hung on. The stallion neighed, pawed at the sky, as if trying to climb off the hateful earth, away from two-legged creatures who wanted to dominate him. When he came down, he turned viciously to bite, but couldn't. Then deliberately he ran close to the fence, to rub her off, forcing her to shift her weight. The stallion, almost diabolic in its cunning, sensed her off balance, went into the air, his body in a corkscrew, which unhinged her further, and she slipped off, went down near the fence. The stallion, who'd gone into a spasm of bucking, finally stopped, turned to look at her, snorted and started to her, but she slipped under the fence.

The crowd groaned when she went down, and Braddock looked relieved that she'd come off that easy.

146

"She's a lucky lady," Fargo said.

"She'll go back," predicted Allen. "She's not a loser."

And to Fargo's astonishment, she did. Dusted herself off, commanded the handlers to set up the stallion again—shook off Braddock, who told her she already had a triumph staying on that long.

Julie's eyes glittered with admiration. "She may not have sense, but she's got guts."

"Guts won't help," Fargo said grimly.

Again the handlers held the horse while she climbed on, and again the stallion stood still, quivering with fury and fear because this hateful creature once again dared to violate his body.

He stood immovable, like a marble horse, until she struck him with her quirt, then he ran at the fence with blinding speed, dug his back legs in and heaved. Though shaken, she clung to him; his teeth bared, he tried to bite again, his ears went up sharply, he neighed, then began to buck viciously, kicking and twisting, turning in tight circles, trying to reach her with his wicked teeth—then he crow-hopped, bumped, heaved.

He went again toward the fence, but the woman grabbed his mane, turned him to the center, struck him with the quirt. The stallion put its last strength into a frenzy of bucking and sky climbing, hooves stabbing at the heavens.

Then, as if he realized the creature on his back couldn't be beat, he went still, absolutely still.

She urged him forward and his teeth bared, but he ran easy round the corral, obeyed her when she wheeled him from one side to the other. His viciousness seemed gone. She laughed, thrilled that she'd defeated an unregenerate beast; the cowboys yelled and whistled.

"I told you," said Allen.

She slipped off the horse, started for Braddock, her face in a smile of triumph. Fargo never stopped watching the stallion; his ears were up, his wild eyes watched the woman, then he trotted gently, as if following her. Fargo felt his flesh crawl.

"Look out," he yelled sharply.

Then the stallion lunged at her, biting at her, pushing her, so that she tumbled, lay helpless while the horse, neighing wildly, rose over her, ready to stomp, but Fargo's gun was pumping bullets and it caught the stallion in midair; he screamed in agony, came down, his hooves missing the prone woman by inches. He fell to his side, his big body heaving, his legs kicking crazily until he went still.

The woman had rolled away, and now she stood, looking white, shaken; she dusted her pants, stared at Fargo and came toward him.

"A rotten heart in that horse," she said. "Thanks."

Braddock hurried over, his face creased with feelings; he was angry yet relieved, angry that he hadn't anticipated what happened, relieved that she'd not been mutilated by the hooves.

"This is Fargo," he said. "Bea Talley. Likes to be called Talley."

"Mr. Fargo," she said, her voice crisp. "I should thank you for saving me from a stompin'. But I confess it's hard to stand the loss of that stallion."

Fargo's face was grim. "Too far to use a lasso. But that stallion had one idea in his head, ma'am, and it was to pound you into the ground."

"How d'ye know that?" Her eyebrows arched.

"I know a killer horse. I've seen them. They come at you gentle and friendly, then kick you to death."

Braddock, listening with tight lips, said, "I'm afraid, Bea, that I have to agree with Fargo. That

148

stallion was a killer horse. I wasn't sure. Just thought him ornery, but I was wrong. Shouldn't let you ride him. I didn't want you to."

She shrugged. "So be it—all's well that ends well. I thank you then." She glanced at Julie, who'd been listening. "And who is this beautiful young lady?"

"Julie Davis," said Fargo, his eyes sharp to watch Braddock. All the foreman did was raise his eyebrows, as a man might do to a beautiful woman.

"Miss Davis, someone like you is rare on this ranch. All we got is a mess of hungry cowboys and some plain-looking janes." The woman studied Julie with a smile.

"I met Fargo last night in a poker game, Bea. He's a clever player."

Bea Talley stared at Braddock. "That means you lost, Brad. Naturally he'd have to be clever to beat you."

"I admit it, I did lose. If I can persuade Fargo and Miss Julie to visit with us a couple of days, I could get revenge."

Bea Talley gazed at Fargo. "They're welcome. Fargo saved me from walking around with a face flat as a pancake. Anything you want, just ask for it. I'm going back to the house to refresh. Why not show Fargo and the lady something of the ranch, Brad?"

"We'd enjoy that," Fargo said, thinking it'd be a good time to close in on Braddock and get some answers at last. But to his surprise, when they started riding over the ranch, five hefty cowboys followed.

The cowboys stayed about thirty yards behind, out of earshot, but always there, always alert.

"Why the escort?" Fargo asked finally.

Braddock shrugged. "Talley's orders. We get

Comanches out here who steal horses, and there are times we need plenty of firepower." His hand swept the horizon. "This ranch is big, Fargo, with a frontage on the river. You can't put a fence around a land like this."

"How big is it?" asked Julie.

Braddock grinned. "Mr. Talley, when alive, was a man with a strong acquisitive instinct. We have twenty thousand head of cattle, about five hundred horses. I remember Mr. Talley saying, 'I got at least twenty miles of the richest land in Texas. And it's all mine.' "

All *mine*. Fargo gazed at the land, its trees, its great meadows, its slopes and its cliffs. He thought of the Comanches. They never said the land was all theirs. It never occurred to them that the land, given by the Great Spirit, could belong to any one man.

As if Braddock was thinking the same thing, he said, "The Comanches don't respect private property, probably don't understand it. That's another reason they cut through this land, apart from wanting to steal horses. And that's why we need five good pistols behind us."

"How long ago did Talley die?" Fargo asked.

"Been only three months. Comanche arrows. He made a helluva fight to stay alive." Braddock shook his head.

Fargo gazed at the great stretch of grazing land in front of them. "A man like that doesn't like to die. And leave all this behind."

Braddock smiled. "Nobody wants to leave all this."

"I expect that makes the Widow Talley the richest catch in Waco," said Fargo.

Braddock grinned. "Yeah, Fargo. You're a good-looking man, but don't get any bright ideas."

Fargo grinned back. "Who me? The lady's too mature. And I'm not a marrying man, just now."

Braddock smiled. "Nice to hear."

Julie's mouth was tight. "Braddock, can I ask, did you ever meet Jed Davis?"

Braddock looked into her eyes. "No, can't say I have. Kin to you?"

"My father."

"Your father! No, never met him." His face became serious. "Why? Did you think I had?"

"I didn't know. Thought you might. Years ago, my father lived somewhere near here."

Braddock looked at her intently. "Why'd you think I might know him? Tell me."

She said nothing, just stared into the distance. Braddock glanced at Fargo.

"Is this . . . was it your family that Joadie shot up?" Braddock asked, his face grim.

She stared, her cheeks aflame.

Fargo spoke quickly. "I told Braddock last night that Joadie had wiped out a family in Eagle Butte. And that Joadie said someone in Waco hired him."

Braddock's jaw was hard. "And you thought it was me! Me! Damn. That's a miserable thing to think, Miss Julie. I didn't know your father, never met him. And if I had a grievance against him, I'd never hire someone to do my dirty work. That Joadie was one ornery polecat. A killer, yes, and a liar down to his bones. Do you know why I ran him out of the ranch? Because he forced young Pete Fulton, a kid, to pull his gun. Because Pete beat him in poker. Shoulda strung Joadie up instead—might have saved your family."

Julie's eyes misted. "Yes, Mr. Braddock, if you had done that, my family would still be alive."

"I'm deeply sorry, Miss Julie," he said, and swung his gelding around. "Let's head back. It's getting near suppertime."

151

8

Fargo's room was big with a thick red rug, a painting, a square mirror over a dresser made of oak.

After washing up, Fargo lay on his soft bed, hands behind his head, and thought about Braddock. The man had to be either innocent as a babe or a great actor. Nothing suggested he was faking, but you couldn't always read the mind of a man. There was a ring of truth in his voice when he told Julie he'd never hire a killer to do his dirty work.

That meant Joadie was a liar. A damned puzzle; Fargo felt that a complicated man like Braddock needed to be pried open, and that could happen only if he got Braddock alone. It was why he told Julie it'd be a good idea to spend a day or two at the ranch. The truth, if there was any, was sunk in this ranch, that was his feeling.

He shut his eyes, smarting from the fierce sun, and dozed till he heard a light tap on the door.

"They're waiting downstairs, Mr. Fargo. It's suppertime." It was the soft voice of Bolton, the manservant.

He went down to a huge dining room with a long table covered with a luxurious tablecloth. The forks and spoons were gleaming silver, the glasses delicate crystal. And there were candles in silver candlesticks. The woman Talley, who was bent to

Julie, listening with a smile, wore an elegant white shirt, tailored riding pants and fancy leather boots. Her light gray hair was set handsomely, and she wore a necklace. She looked to Fargo like a woman who'd once been beautiful, but who time was slowly eroding away. Next to her Braddock sat, wearing a red shirt, a shoelace tie under a black vest.

Bea Talley, when she saw Fargo, stopped talking to Julie and smiled. "Ah, the man who saved me from a killer stallion. Can I thank you again, Fargo. Bolton," she told the butler, "pour Mr. Fargo some champagne. We get it shipped in from New Orleans."

Bolton, a remarkably big, broad-shouldered man with alert brown eyes, poured champagne. Fargo lifted it, inclined his head to her and sipped it. Bubbly stuff, with a nice taste, but not his idea of a drink with a kick.

"Yes, Fargo," the lady went on, "I begin to realize how foolish I was to try and tame that stallion."

"It's the kind of horse," Fargo said, "that can't be dominated, can't be tamed, can't be broken." He stared into her light blue eyes. "There are horses like that, and men too. You turn horses loose because they can't live in captivity." He paused. "I don't know what you do with the men." He glanced at Braddock, who kept his eyes on his handsome lady.

She smiled ironically. "But most men are tamable. Don't you think so, Miss Julie?"

Julie smiled. "I don't have much experience. But Fargo doesn't look like he could be tamed."

The lady's blue eyes studied Fargo. "I don't deny that he's something like a panther. But tamable, if the right woman got a hold." She turned to Braddock. "Now here's a red-blooded man. He's like a lion

153

with the other men. But like a lamb when he comes to me. Aren't you, Brad?"

Braddock shifted in his chair, then lifted his glass. "Bea, I suspect there's not a man in Texas you couldn't turn into a lamb."

Fargo, looking at him, felt that in her hands he was a pussycat. He seemed overpowered by either her personality or her ranch.

Julie seemed to be fascinated by Talley. "Why'd you want to ride a stallion like that anyway? He looked like the meanest brute in the corral."

Bea Talley's blue eyes were stony. "That was why, Julie. Just because he was the meanest. There's glory in that." She turned to Fargo. "Don't you agree?"

Fargo smiled grimly. She was a ball-breaker, this one. "People find glory in different things."

She sensed his attitude. "What do you find glory in, Fargo?"

He raised his glass. "I don't think about it."

Bolton brought out a big dish and spooned soup into their bowls. It tasted like potato soup but was delicately flavored, and Fargo liked it.

Bea Talley kept looking at Fargo. "What'd you think of the ranch?"

"It's like owning half of Texas," he said.

She laughed. "Mr. Talley liked to collect things. He collected cattle, horses, money and land."

"Seems to have collected you too," Fargo said.

"No, Mr. Fargo, I collected him." Her eyes were cool. "Nobody collects me, you see. I was not a poor girl when my father, Charlie Fremont, died. I had some money, and Mr. Talley was just beginning. He was very busy thinking how to become a rich man. Too busy, even, to think about a wife. I had to get hold of him, shake him up, tell him that with my money he could buy big land with river frontage, some cattle and horses and start breeding. If there was one thing Mr. Talley liked, it was a woman who had ideas on how to make money grow. I collected him, you see. And he was very happy counting all the things he owned till the day of his death." Her eyes clouded, and she reached for her glass.

"Doesn't sound very romantic," Julie said. "But very clever."

"Life isn't just romance," the lady said in a tight voice. "Romance is just dreams, and dreams can hurt."

There was a moment of silence, while everyone looked at her. Then Bolton came in with a great roast. He cut thick slices and put the browned meat with the pink center on each place, then spooned out the yams, corn and black-eyed peas.

"This is a great ranch," said Braddock. "Wish we could persuade you to join us, Fargo. We could use a man like you."

Talley waited, it seemed to Fargo, eagerly for his answer.

"I've got a couple of things to do before I can strike roots," Fargo said.

She studied him. "You're tracking someone. Is that it?"

His jaw was hard. "Some men broke into my home and killed my family. I can never rest until they've been paid off. The same thing happened to Julie's family. I wonder if you know."

Bea Talley looked as if she'd been wounded. "Yes, Brad was telling me. I didn't care to bring it up. A terrible, terrible thing." She paused. "What I found amazing was that you came here, to Waco, to find someone. On the word of Joadie Smith."

"What do you mean?" asked Julie.

The woman folded her hands tightly and spoke slowly. "Joadie Smith was a yellow dog, a filthy liar and a killer of kids. He killed Pete Fulton, forced him into a gunfight and killed him. Pete, a sweet youngster of seventeen, who had his life ahead of him. I told Brad that Joadie Smith should be strung up like a pig. But they couldn't hang him because Pete did draw his gun. Then I told Brad to run him off the ranch, right away. And he did. Joadie Smith was broke, picked up with a couple of drifters and went looking for money. He found it, I believe, at your house. It was a tragedy."

Fargo stared at her; an extraordinary woman, powerful, complicated.

"But," Braddock said, "Joadie got his. Fargo caught up with him."

"What I didn't understand," said Fargo, "is why Joadie Smith said he'd been hired by someone in Waco."

"By Braddock, you mean," Talley said. "That's what you mean, isn't it? Why shouldn't Joadie Smith say it. He wanted to get back at Braddock. Hoped you'd cut down Braddock for him. A crazy story. Joadie Smith was a thief, a liar and a killer. You don't take the word of a man like that. Do you, Fargo?" She waited, then again: "Do you?"

He stared at her. She wanted him to say something, she wanted to know if he believed her. And suddenly, because she wanted it, he made the decision not to say it. Just to see what would happen. "I've learned, Mrs. Talley, that the truth is one of the hardest things in the world to discover."

Her eyes were cold as blue ice, and she turned to glance at Braddock. "We'll have coffee on the terrace, Bolton," she said.

From that moment, she treated him formally, as if he was no longer of interest. Instead she warmed up to Julie, smiled at her, paid her compliments. Fargo watched, amused. She had to win, and if it couldn't be Fargo, it'd be the girl.

Later, Fargo walked about, under the big stars, trying to put it together. Something mysterious was going on, but he couldn't put a finger on it. He felt that strongly.

Was Braddock guilty after all, and was Talley trying to whitewash him?

Answers were to be found here, but he didn't know where.

A curious thought crept into his mind; it wasn't clear yet. Tomorrow, he'd dig around a bit.

Next day, early, after a restless night, Fargo mounted the Ovaro and rode east. There were times, after he'd been crowded by people, when he craved the open spaces, the sky above him, the trees around him. He needed just one companion, his magnificent pinto.

He rode the trail through a flat plain and looked with pleasure at the jagged profile of a far-off peak, the green cluster of pines, the stretch of tall grass. The sun at the horizon was a half ball of fire, shooting out orange fingers to the sky. He could hear the creak of his saddle and the scrabble of a marmot. A hawk soared overhead, its eye keen for breakfast.

Fargo's mind kept touching on Talley. Something nagged him, but he couldn't spell it out. Clearly she was involved with Braddock. He was her number-one man, and she cared about him, though she treated him lightly. She wanted nothing to happen to him. Fargo patted the flank of the pinto, startled by the move of a coyote in the brush. No, the Widow Talley seemed to worry about what he might try to do to her dear friend Braddock. Maybe she figured the man who had mowed down Joadie and his friends was dangerous and could damage someone she cared about. That could explain her actions. Probably she told Braddock to hire him; once on the ranch he'd be bought off; if not that, he'd be under her thumb.

Fargo smiled—fat chance.

The sun had climbed, and he could feel its heat—another scorcher. He headed to the cool of the pines where he had picked up the rippling sound of water.

No, he thought, Talley couldn't buy him off; but not to agree with her last night seemed to have triggered something in her. She was a hardheaded woman who wanted her way, in fact, couldn't stand not to have it. All this power and land, Fargo thought, made her think she could dominate the lives of others. Funny how once he blocked her, she stopped trying to charm him and began to work on Julie. Yes, she had to win at something.

The big trees around him sent out a strong scent of pine, and he nudged the pinto along the trail toward the bubbling sound of water. When the pinto's ears went up, Fargo thought thirst was the cause, but the horse must have known about the water long ago. Fargo's body alerted, and just then he heard the whisper of a branch, sensed the body falling, saw the shining gleam of steel. His arm came up to stop the downward thrust of the arm, and he felt the impact of the bronze body, colliding with him, knocking him off the saddle. They fell to earth, the muscular body of the Comanche on top. Fargo could see the red, blunt face, the fierce brown eyes as the Comanche tried to grab his throat with his left hand and force down the knife with the other. His arm was powerful, and it took every ounce of Fargo's strength to stop its downward movement. He gripped at the fingers trying for his throat, twisting until he heard fingers snap. No sound of pain came from the Comanche, though his hand had become useless; Fargo concentrated on the knife hand, only two inches from his heart. Their bodies were frozen in strain, as Fargo stared into the Comanche's eyes, seeing neither hate nor fear, just determination to kill. This Comanche had saved him from Burt's hangmen just so he could personally kill Fargo. He smelled the tart sweat of the redskin, felt the straining muscles of his body, saw the veins in his thick neck like cords as he tried to force the knife down. They stayed locked arm to arm; then Fargo, in a sudden move, using all his strength, heaved the Comanche over, twisting the knife hand until the wrist bones cracked and the knife fell.

He grabbed the knife, flung it into the bushes, then stood up, bringing out his gun.

The Comanche, his eyes dull, rose slowly to his feet, his head high, face impassive, waited for the bullet to end his life.

Fargo took a deep breath, then said in dialect, "Is it right to make war on Fargo?"

The Comanche looked at his fingers, broken and useless. "Shoot. I wait to join my fathers."

"Again, I ask, is it right to make war on Fargo?"

The Comanche spoke slowly. "I am the last kinsman of Red Wolf."

Fargo stared at him. The Comanche had no fear of death; he would join the great spirits of his ancestors, he had acted nobly.

"What are you called?"

The Indian, who couldn't be more than twenty, spoke proudly. "I am called Running Fox."

"Running Fox, you shot the paleface who would have killed Fargo?"

Running Fox let the ghost of a smile cross his lips. "Yes, to save you for death by a Comanche. But it is Running Fox who will die." Their eyes met, and Fargo could see no fear, just a willingness to die—without cowardice.

He spoke slowly. "I killed Red Wolf because he would kill Soft Cloud, one of the Comanche sisters. She would not be his squaw. It is right for a woman to choose. And now Soft Cloud is dead. It is useless to war further. You have saved my life, Running Fox. I give you yours. I ask you not to war again on Fargo. Will you give your word?"

There was a long moment as Running Fox thought, his eyes glowing with feeling.

Then a small smile came to his lips. "Fargo has bad enemies. I have seen them. Running Fox gives Fargo his word." With that, he put his hand over his heart, looked full into Fargo's eyes, wheeled and moved like a shadow into the pines and was gone.

Fargo stood silent, thinking. There was nobility and strength in this Comanche. He was young. Running Fox. It would not be surprising if he became a warrior chief someday.

9

As the pinto jogged toward the ranch Fargo thought of the Comanche and his clever stakeout. From a high position, the Indian had seen the direction he was riding the pinto and figured in this heat he'd take the trail to water. So he positioned himself over the trail in a thickly branched tree and waited for the paleface to pass under it.

All predictable, and it was lucky the pinto's ears went up. With its keen sense of vision and smell, the pinto had given him many a warning moments before attack. He couldn't count the times the pinto had saved his life. He rubbed the flank of the horse affectionately, and as if in recognition, the pinto threw up his head and neighed. Fargo smiled; it was mutual love.

As he approached the terrace behind the house, covered with a yellow awning, he could see Julie and Talley at the table. They were sipping from long cool glasses. Talley watched him for a few moments as he rode toward them, then spoke to Julie and went into the house.

By the time Fargo reached the table, Bolton had appeared. "Would Mr. Fargo care for a cool drink?"

Fargo mopped his brow. "Some rye and water," he said.

Julie smiled at him, then frowned. "You look like you've been knocking down a tree."

He grunted. "More like knocking down a Comanche," he said. Just then he noticed Braddock, who'd come from the other side of the house, ride at a quick canter toward the bunks. Fargo watched him for a moment.

Julie's eyes opened wide. "What do you mean, 'Comanche'?"

He shrugged and drank part of the whiskey Bolton had put down. "Comanches don't recognize private ownership of land, as you heard."

"Are you hurt?"

"Everything's all right."

"What about the Comanche?"

"His name was Running Fox. Young, but tough. Saved me from hanging in Lemon Creek. So I let him go."

She frowned. "Was that smart? He may come after you again."

"He gave his word. The Comanche keeps his word." He glanced at the door. "I noticed that Talley made a quick run when she saw me coming. Not her favorite guest, am I?"

Julie's eyes glowed. "You're wrong about that, Fargo. She admires you. She wishes you'd accept Braddock's offer. They'd give you a responsible job. To help run the ranch."

Fargo grimaced. "She's *too* generous."

Julie didn't notice his irony. "Oh yes, she is. She's a warmhearted woman, Fargo. I didn't care for her at first. But I know her better now. She's very generous."

Fargo looked at his glass. "How so?"

Julie leaned to him. "She feels the kind of pain that I've gone through. About the family. She knows what it is, she says, to be without kinfolk, to be alone. She'd like me to stay on the ranch. She'd find something I liked to do. Don't you think that generous?"

Fargo was surprised: it *was* generous. Talley seemed to be a woman who made up her mind in a hurry. Well, Julie was a lovely young woman, and it might be just right for her to be in a place like this. She'd be protected, she'd have a home base.

"Sounds good, Julie."

"I told her I'd think about it. Wanted your opinion." Her lovely face looked mournful. "There's nothing left for me in Eagle Butte. Nothing. I have to start my life over. This might be a good place."

"What about Braddock?"

She shook her head. "Talley tells me that Braddock is four-square, worth his weight in gold. I tend to believe her. She says that Joadie lied, hoped you'd come here and get Braddock for him. Because he hated Braddock's guts. It adds up, doesn't it?"

"Maybe it does." He glanced at the horizon, and it jarred him to see Braddock again, this time riding toward the north corral. He watched the way he rode, tall in the saddle, strong, and it struck him that for once Braddock was riding alone.

He reached out to Julie's hand. "I'll be back shortly."

It took twenty minutes of riding to move within five hundred yards of Braddock, whose gelding moved at an easy pace. Braddock's destination was not clear, for he shifted direction twice. Now he turned sharply to the higher ground, a land thick with cottonwoods and shrubs. Perhaps behind this were cattle grazing grounds. It looked like a smart time to get Braddock alone and see if he could get some truth out of him. Maybe he was in the clear, but Fargo needed more than just a declaration of innocence to prove it. He felt again something was off tilt in this ranch.

Braddock had gone into a densely wooded area, and now they were miles from the ranch buildings. Fargo went alert; land like this, he knew, lent itself to ambush, and anything could be lurking: Braddock, Running Fox, even another Comanche.

It was this alertness that made him aware that someone was tracking, not behind him, but parallel to him, on his left. The delicate movement of a branch was all he needed. Casually he swung off the pinto and began to walk quietly, his eyes moving restlessly, his ears tuned to a whisper of sound. Might be Braddock, who somehow had doubled back and was trying for position. Position for what? Shooting? Fargo stroked his chin; that's what he had to find out. If Braddock took a shot, then he was guilty as hell; he had hired Joadie and should be exterminated like a rat.

Then the gun roared and the bullet whizzed past Fargo's head, an inch away, and Fargo wheeled left, fired where the branch moved. A cry of pain, the toppling of a body. Fargo crouched, inched ahead, pushing brush and branches aside, then he heard the roar of a gun again, but this time no bullet came at him. Still he dived to the ground, waited, heard a thrashing sound, began to crawl forward, staying low. But the going was hard—roots, dead trunks and bushes. Finally he glimpsed a brown vest and a man sprawled, facedown. Fargo listened—nothing; he moved to the man, turned him. A dark, bearded face with dead shocked brown eyes looked up— Allen. Fargo was jolted. The body had two wounds, in the shoulder and chest. Fargo's eyes searched the surrounding trees, bushes—no sound, no movement. He reached for Allen's gun—one bullet fired. He looked at the earth—fresh tracks, in fact, Braddock's tracks. He knew them because he always looked at tracks, to him they were clear as faces.

Fargo moved in a crouch. Braddock, obviously, had shot Allen, finished him off; that was the second shot. Why? Because he didn't want Allen, only wounded, saying the wrong thing. What the hell was Allen doing there?

No need to spell that out. When he was on the terrace with Julie, Braddock, in clear sight, started to ride alone with one aim: to pull him into ambush by Allen.

What the hell did it mean?

Braddock wanted him out, that's what it meant. Fargo studied the prints; Braddock had gone quickly, almost on toes, toward the densest part of the thicket, in case Fargo followed.

Why'd Braddock want him out? Because he'd gotten too close, because he didn't buy the story about Joadie. Well, he had Braddock cornered, and it was time to choke the whole truth out of that big, beefy bastard.

Gun ready, he moved after Braddock's tracks.

He crouched and moved step by step into the dense thicket, ears strained to catch sound; in tangled terrain like this, it'd be almost impossible to move without sound.

Though he tried never to step on a twig, always on soft earth, it seemed he made the only sound. A sudden scuttling caused his flesh to crawl, even though his mind read it instantly as a marmot. But the fears of a waiting gunman were triggered, for a gun roared and bullets thudded wildly into tree trunks. Fargo fired twice, and a groan told him he'd scored a hit. Fearful that his bullet might have been deadly—he needed a living Braddock to get answers—Fargo, in a crouch, moved fast to the point of the groan. Expecting it to be Braddock, he was jarred to find instead one of the men who had stood behind Braddock during the poker game. He lay on the ground, a bullet in his throat, the blood gushing like a fountain. With agony in his eyes, he looked at Fargo, unable to speak, aware his lifeblood was pouring out. Then his eyes closed.

Fargo gritted his teeth. Had he been tracking this man, thinking him Braddock? No, he never made mistakes like that. He had been tracking Braddock, who brought him into ambush with a backup gunman in case the first one fizzled. Were there more? Braddock had to be near; he'd shot Allen to shut him up, laid down a clear trail to bring him past this gunman. He had to be near. How to smoke him out, that was the trick. Somewhere in this dense thicket, Braddock waited. He wouldn't move, not until he heard the voice of his gunman; and hearing nothing, he had to figure Fargo was still alive and prowling.

How, Fargo wondered, could he get a fix on his position? Would he fall for the old Indian trick of a sudden movement from a stone tossed through the bushes? Wouldn't hurt to try.

No stone, but there were twigs, dead branches. He bent noiselessly, lifted a twig and lofted it to fall through the branches of a cottonwood ahead.

He heard it—a quick, soft move to the front and left, near a thick tree trunk. Braddock, or whoever lurked there, was startled by the sound but not pushed into wild firing. But he had betrayed his position. Now the trick was to move noiselessly and get behind that tree trunk.

Fargo studied the trunk, the surrounding ground, printed it in his mind, moved back soundlessly and worked in a great circle, taking more than twenty minutes to reach the position where he could see Braddock's tree from behind. Quietly he peered through the heavy leaves, the thick branches, and made out the big, bulking body of Braddock pressed against the trunk, his gun held ready.

Fargo always believed that the instinct to survive is so powerful its mystery can't be explained. Fargo hadn't moved, hadn't made a sound, yet the man he was looking at suddenly turned to stare behind him, and his shocked blue eyes locked on Fargo's. Quick as a flash, he swung his gun around, but Fargo fired, and Braddock's gun jumped from his fingers. He shook his hand, as if it had gone numb.

Fargo moved in on him, his gun ready, his eyes glittering ice points.

Braddock suddenly smiled; he was a smiling man, even in front of a gun. "You're a tough man, Fargo. A little indestructible. I can understand why they couldn't knock you off."

Fargo came in close, stared hard at the broad-boned face, then picked up his gun, threw it into the bushes. "Start the story from the beginning," he said. "With Joadie."

Braddock grinned. "Listen, Fargo, all you're doing is shooting up a lotta men. And you're not a dime richer. Does that make sense? I can make you rich. Take twenty grand in gold—and go anywhere you want. Just forget about us."

"Forget about who?"

Braddock's eyes veiled. "Why ask questions? What difference will it make? I can put together twenty thousand for you. In gold. We'll work out guarantees, so that you get away—safe and sound. Say yes, and by tonight, you can be on your way, with the gold."

Fargo's lake-blue eyes drilled into him. "Just start from the beginning, Braddock."

Braddock shook his head and looked down. His shoelace was loose. "You're a stubborn man." He bent to lace his shoe. Just then, as if on cue, a small animal scrambled past madly, and at the sound, Fargo turned to look. Braddock had incredible luck, for he had just scuffed dirt, and in the same movement flung it at Fargo's eyes, following with a running butt in his gut.

Fargo fell back, his eyes gritty with dirt, his wind knocked out. His gun loosened and Braddock, with remarkable alertness, kicked at it, spinning the gun twenty feet away.

Braddock started toward the gun, but Fargo, in spite of his pain, grabbed at Braddock's ankle, jerked him off balance and he hit the ground. It took about five seconds for both of them to rise and face each other.

Braddock grinned. "Well, Fargo, you don't want to be rich, so you'll be dead. I'm going to do it with my fists." And he showed his fists, like big meat packs.

Blinking his eyes in an effort to clear them, Fargo turned to face Braddock. He was big-chested, with huge biceps, a broad-boned face, a thick neck and vicious fists built for slugging men into submission. His grin was devilish. "You interfered from the beginning—and this is the end of the trail for you, Fargo. But I'm not a hard man, so I'm going to finish you off fast. You won't know what hit you."

He moved in, his massive fists in front of him, feinted and swung. Fargo, still not clear-eyed and nauseous in his gut from the butting, tried to shift away but didn't escape the punch, which caught the side of his head. The shock of the blow went right through him and he stood petrified; Braddock swung again, a blow at his jaw. It sent Fargo reeling and he almost sat down. Braddock laughed, convinced it would be easy to destroy this man.

Because of that, he stopped to talk. "See, Fargo, without a gun, you're nothing. Just a stupid meddler whose luck has run out." He shook his head in pity. "You might have had a bag of gold." He grinned devilishly. "But then again, you might not. We're not stupid, you know."

Fargo shook his head, now cleared, and his eyes too. This cocky idiot could have done a lot of damage if he hadn't stopped to crow. Fargo stood there, as if dazed, waiting for Braddock. He did come in, lined up for a thundering right to Fargo's jaw, when Fargo's fist shot out and smashed his nose. His head went back and the blood spurted red. Fargo, crouching, threw two hard, lightning punches at Braddock's gut, and grunted. Braddock's eyes narrowed. "Sneaky bastard, we'll take care of you."

He rushed, throwing wild, ponderous punches, one grazing Fargo's cheek, jolting him. Fargo danced away, feinted, crashed a right to Braddock's jaw, followed with two more fast rights that rocked the beefy man. He stood stunned a moment, the power of Fargo's fists made him realize he was in a fight. The scoffing look had slipped off his face, and he settled down to serious fighting.

He swung hard at Fargo's head; Fargo blocked it partly but was jarred. He countered with a driving right and left to Braddock's gut, then another hard right to his nose, to draw fresh blood, another to his eye. Braddock was jarred, and he crouched and swung a blow as low as he could. Fargo's gut felt as if it would explode; he fell back. Braddock, seeing victory, rushed forward, and Fargo, summoning all his strength, kicked at Braddock's groin; with a guttural scream, he went down.

Fargo looked at him, walked to his gun and came back. Braddock still lay doubled up on the ground, squirming, moaning, holding his groin.

Fargo watched without pity. This man had tried to ambush him; he was the man behind the death of Julie's family. A kick in the balls was too good for him.

He sat on a dead tree trunk and waited. It took twenty minutes for Braddock to come around. He looked beat, his face greenish, his nose bloody, his eye swollen red.

Fargo walked in front of him. "You hired Joadie, didn't you?"

Braddock looked at him, still greenish, but said nothing.

Fargo cocked his gun. "You still got your life to lose. I can shoot. And bury you here. Nobody will ever know."

Braddock stared into those stony blue eyes and realized Fargo might do it. He sighed deeply. "Yes, I hired Joadie."

"Why?"

Braddock found it hard to talk. He wiped his nose. "To get rid of them. The Davis family."

"Why? What the hell did Davis ever do to you?"

Braddock looked up, surprised. "Me? He didn't do nothing to me."

Fargo stared. "What do you mean? There was an old feud between you both. Wasn't there?"

Braddock again wiped his nose, looked painfully at the blood. "Naw. No feud. Did it for her."

"Her!" It was an amazing moment. It took some

time before Fargo could grasp the meaning, then suddenly he felt the buck could be passed no more, that the truth was out. Her.

"Her? You mean Talley."

Braddock nodded. "That's it, Talley."

"Why—for God's sake?"

"Ask her." Braddock's eyes were half closed.

"I'm asking you."

He shook his head. "I don't know why. She never told me why. But I figured if she wanted it done, she had to have a hell of a good reason. I mean Bea Talley wouldn't want to do a thing like that for no reason. She's not like that."

Fargo thought about it, then slowly nodded. This had to be the truth. Because Talley was the kind of woman with the iron to make a decision like that—to execute a family!

He nodded. "Okay, Braddock, I'm taking you in. You've got a lot to answer for. But you'll get justice." He smiled grimly. "Probably at the end of a rope."

Braddock's eyes glinted wickedly, but he said nothing.

Fargo's jaw hardened as a thought struck him. "Let's get the horses." They picked up the pinto first, then Braddock's gelding.

Fargo watched Braddock through slitted eyes as he shuffled in his saddlebag, a mite too long. Then he wheeled about, his Colt in his hand.

Fargo's move was quicker, for his gun fired almost as it cleared its holster, the bullet hurtling into Braddock's body. He fell like a dead log, facedown.

10

The sun was almost at the horizon and the sky an ocean of flame when he reached the big white building. Talley was nowhere in sight; her sorrel was gone. He went to Julie's room, tapped lightly on the door; she opened it and looked at him, her lovely face furrowed with anxiety. He walked past her to the water basin, washed his face and toweled it.

"Fargo," she said, the pain in her eyes. "Is there no end to this? All the fighting."

He put the towel down and sat in the chair, aware now of a lot of aches and pains in his body and face.

"You went after Braddock," she said. "I saw you."

He nodded.

"Where is Braddock?"

"Dead," Fargo said. "With two of his men he set up to bushwhack me."

Her face paled. "Good God! Braddock!" Her green eyes were wide with shock. "Braddock! But why did he do that?"

"Because Talley told him, that's why."

Her eyes glittered with disbelief. "Fargo, Fargo. It's been too much for you. All this killing. You're losing your grip. Bea would never do a thing like that. I told you, she's everything gentle, kind, loving. I don't believe it."

He grimaced. "Bea? She's done a great job on you, Julie. But I've got the truth now. She's the one. The one behind it all. I squeezed it out of Braddock. She ordered him to send Joadie up to Eagle Butte—to wipe out your family."

Julie's hand went to her breast as if she'd been stabbed, her face distorted with pain. "It can't be true, Fargo, it can't. He had some devil's reason to blame her. She'd never do a thing like that. I tell you, she's a gentle woman, a kind woman."

There was a long silence.

"She's the only one with the guts to do it," Fargo said, suddenly thinking of the way Talley tried to crush the spirit of the stallion. "Remember how she was with the stallion."

There was another long silence.

Why she did it, had the family wiped out, Fargo didn't understand. The woman, the boy—it was still a monstrous mystery.

Julie was thinking hard, Fargo could tell. She had to be remembering her terrible loss because suddenly an iron hardness came to her face. She walked to the wall where her gun holster hung, strapped it about her waist.

"Let's get to the bottom of this, Fargo, right now."

They went downstairs and called Bolton.

"We'd like to see Mrs. Talley," Fargo said politely.

Bolton pointed through the window. "She's just riding in from the west corral." They went out to the terrace while he watched her ride a big handsome sorrel, then swing off it gracefully.

She seemed preoccupied and stared at Fargo, obviously at the bruises on his face, but made no reference to them. She walked to the whiskey bottles on the long table. "Let's have some drinks," she said, her voice taut. She poured liquor into three glasses and sat, looking at them. "A blister of a day," she said. "Will this heat ever end?" She emptied her glass. "I have a bad thirst." She poured another, sipped part of it.

Then she looked at Fargo. "I wonder if Julie told you how much we'd like you to join us? I know you're a traveling man. But there's a big job opening here. The top job in fact. You see"—she looked coy—"I'm going to marry Braddock. Finally. And that leaves the foreman job open. Not many qualify for that. But I think you're right for it. I can tell about men." She glanced at Julie affectionately. "Julie is thinking of staying with us too. It'd be wonderful. We'd all be together. What do you say?"

Fargo put his hand around his glass, his eyes frosty. "I'm afraid, Mrs. Talley, it's too late to marry Braddock."

She stared at him as if she didn't hear him, her face puzzled. "What? What did you say? I didn't hear that."

He stared deep into her eyes. "I said it was too late to marry Braddock."

Her features hardened. "I thought you said that. What the hell do you mean?"

Fargo kept looking into her blue clouded eyes. "Braddock's dead."

She recoiled as if she'd been hit. Her eyes locked onto his.

"Dead. Brad? Dead." Her hand moved to her breast, which began to heave. "How'd it—who . . ."

Fargo's mouth was a tight line. "He tried to bushwhack me, with two men. They're all dead."

There was a long silence. Bea Talley sat as if turned to stone. Julie studied her.

"The game's up," Fargo said.

"Bolton!" Talley's voice was harsh.

The broad-shouldered man stepped through the door, about to bring his gun up, but Fargo already had the whiskey bottle hurtling through the air at him. It crashed against him, throwing him off balance, and he fell. Fargo's gun was out. Julie's gun was out too, pointing not at Bolton but at Bea Talley.

"You killed my family," she said, her voice hoarse. "And you're going to pay."

Talley stared at her, with pale face, then reached for another whiskey bottle, poured a drink for herself, gulped it down.

Julie watched her with merciless eyes. "What the hell kind of a woman are you?" Her voice was still hoarse. "I thought you were wonderful. I never met anyone like you. But you're not a woman. Some kind of mad, murdering female wolf! Why did you have my family killed? What have they done to you? You don't even know us."

Talley just stared at her, all her defenses stripped away, her eyes big, filled with fear, but she couldn't speak.

"There are at least eight people dead—because of you," Fargo said. "Not counting Julie's father, mother, and brother. Why'd you tell Braddock to wipe out Julie's family? What are you? Who the hell are you?"

There was again that hellish moment of silence. The woman's face now was a mask of stone.

"I'm Julie's mother," she said in a dead voice.

The words fell into a sink of silence. Nobody moved, nobody breathed—and the words hung in the air as if they had no place to go.

Julie's face was drained of color. "What'd you say?" she stammered.

The woman looked at her with hungry eyes. "I'm

your mother, Julie, your *natural* mother. Do you understand?" She paused. "One night, years ago, your father, Jed Davis, curse his black heart, grabbed you, stole five thousand dollars from my safe, and ran off with Millie Jordon, a friend of mine."

Talley lifted the liquor glass in front of her, drank it all.

"Millie Jordon and Jed—they ran away with my baby. And I couldn't have any more children." She stopped, clenched her fists. "I was robbed of motherhood. I searched for him everywhere. I was frantic. Nearly went crazy. Probably I was crazy for a while. Then I swore an oath—that if I ever caught up with them, I'd make them pay—in blood." She seemed to grow calmer, and sipped more liquor.

"I met Talley and put all my heart and energy into becoming rich and powerful, so that someday I could get my revenge. Because all through the years, this thing festered in my mind.

"After Talley died, I was alone. I told Braddock what I wanted. Braddock and I became lovers. We had men searching everywhere for Jed Davis. The fool was too stupid even to change his name. Thought he'd be safe in a hideaway near Eagle Butte. But he was found. Then I told Braddock to take care of it. To destroy Jed Davis and Millie Jordon. They were to do it when you were not there. The boy was not to be touched. But he may have tried to shoot and they gunned him down too." She looked tenderly at Julie. "They were to bring you back here, where we'd arrange to rescue you, one way or another."

She looked tenderly at the young woman in front of her. "Julie, Julie, my only child. We've been long years without each other. But we still have time. I've built this great place for us. It's yours. I've made out my will putting it all in your hands. You

176

must come here and live with me. It's what I've been waiting for, all my life."

Fargo looked at Julie. She was white as a ghost. She had dropped limply to the chair, her green eyes fixed on the woman as if seeing her the first time. Looking from Julie to Talley, Fargo was struck by the points of likeness, the same body frame, same oval face, same nose, same upper lip. No doubt about it, they were the same brand.

So Talley had been behind the whole thing. Suddenly he remembered Burt, in Lemon Creek, dying with an arrow in his chest. "Who put you up to this?" he'd asked, and Burt said, "Tell Lee." *Tell Lee* really meant *Talley*. That damned name stuck in his mind, and was one of the pieces he tried to put together. An iron woman, this one with fire in her heart, who couldn't start living until she had her revenge.

She'd been shrewd, cunning, she had tried to bribe away his suspicions about Joadie with a job on the ranch. When that didn't work and she felt he'd be trouble, she plotted with Braddock.

Yes, she'd plotted the whole thing. If Joadie had brought Julie to Waco, they'd probably have destroyed him, liberated Julie. A grateful Julie would be softened, and Talley, one way or another, would manage to bring her into the ranch. It was Fargo who kept muddling up her plans. He had mowed down Joadie and his two men, then Burt and his two men. Finally it was she who plotted with Braddock how to bring Fargo into ambush, seeing they couldn't buy him off.

Iron woman, she'd stop at nothing to get her daughter. She'd gone too far to stop.

He looked at Julie. Her mind too was working like a machine, thinking of all who were dead because of this vengeful woman. And among the dead were the people she loved.

Bea Talley watched Julie, saw the green of her eyes deepen as she played back everything that happened in her mind. She looked at her newfound mother.

"What do you say, Julie, dear? I've got a mother's love to give you—and all this." She motioned to the ranch around them.

Julie took a deep breath, then finally spoke. "So you're my mother. Yes, I felt something. I felt close to you. And wanted to stay at this beautiful place and be near you. I thought you were wonderful." She shook her head. "But now, all I feel for you is pity. Pity that your hate forced you to do what you did. No, I can't stay here with you. You've done too much."

Bea Talley's face, Fargo saw, was white as a sheet. "You must stay!" she cried. "Don't you realize that everything I've done was for you? It was because I loved you. It's all been for you. You must stay!"

"Stay? After what you did to my family?"

"But I *am* your family. Millie Jordon was not your mother!"

"But Jed Davis was my father."

"Your father? Is it right for a father to steal a baby from its mother? A father like that doesn't deserve to live. You *must* stay here, Julie. It's where you belong. Don't you see—everything I've done has been to bring us together? You can't leave me now. You must live with me." Her voice rang with passion.

"Do you think," Julie spoke slowly, "that I can live with my father's *murderer*?" Her eyes shone like hard green marbles; her tone was implacable.

Bea Talley stood absolutely still, watching as Julie glanced at Fargo and started out to her horse.

He followed, looking back at Talley. She stood silent, as if carved out of stone.

They reached their horses, swung over them. They started to ride. Fargo felt a cool wind playing about his face. Looked like the heat spell finally had been broken.

Then he heard the shot. He flattened against the horse, pulled his gun and turned.

Bea Talley was lying on the ground, and even from here he could see blood trickling from the side of her head.

The sky looked like a blooded orange as Fargo stood, tall and lean, beside Julie. Nearby, the pinto chafed, as if it knew it was time to go and wished Fargo would hurry. There were places to see, mountains to climb, races to be run.

Fargo glanced at the pinto, amused by the way it picked up his feelings.

Then he looked at Julie.

She was looking much better than she did three days ago when Talley had put a bullet in her head.

"I've lost my mother twice," she said to Fargo, in the terrible day afterward. She grieved for Talley as she had grieved for her family.

It had been impossible for her to leave. The Talley ranch was a huge property—land, cattle and horses. The law firm in Waco, Rogers and Dunay, insisted that Julie Davis couldn't walk away from the ranch. They told her she was Talley's rightful and only heir, her acknowledged blood daughter. She would have to stay, claim ownership and take responsibility.

It was to her a disturbing situation, but as Fargo pointed out, she had nowhere else to go.

"Might as well stay," he said.

"Why don't you stay too, Fargo?" she asked. "Like the princess says in the story books, 'half my kingdom is yours.' Please stay."

"Can't stay," Fargo said, his mouth grim. "Your family is avenged. But not mine. I can't rest easy until they are."

She threw her arms around him, kissed him, and her eyes were wet. "Come back anytime."

He smiled at her, swung over the pinto who threw his head, glad to be again moving.

She watched him ride for a long time, until she could hardly see him, a lone rider silhouetted against the blood-red sky.

LOOKING FORWARD

**The following is the opening section
from the next novel in the exciting Trailsman
series from Signet:**

The Trailsman #26
WARPAINT RIFLES

*South Dakota, early 1860s, north of
the Cheyenne River and east of
the Black Hills, a tinderbox land
where savage fury could erupt
at any time . . .*

Even the moon seemed to be waiting.

Almost full, it made the land a place of silver and long shadows. It hung low, as if watching and waiting for hunter and hunted. The leaves of the tanbark oaks hung unmoving, unstirred in the still air. The night creatures stayed motionless. It was a waiting night.

The big man with the lake-blue eyes crouched beside the Ovaro, hardly breathing as he waited. A hundred yards down the hillside, unseen now in the night brush, the others waited. Ten. Big, bronzed, near-naked bodies. Ten Crow bucks, and Skye Fargo's lips drew into a thin line as he asked himself the question again. Why did they wait? Why had they come here to the top of this valley in the night to wait?

His eyes narrowed as he thought back but a few hours earlier. He had picked up the ten Indians as he'd ridden north after he'd crossed the Cheyenne River. He'd spotted them in time to take cover, stay behind and out of sight, a matter of simple self-protection at first. Crow, he had noted, tall, proud, even insolent, each sitting his horse as though he were a king. Two wore wrist gauntlets with Crow markings. And he had seen something else, war paint on faces and chests. He continued to stay back but followed and he had begun to frown. They rode almost in a direct line and two Conestoga wagons came into view. They only paused to look down on them and rode on and Fargo remembered how his frown had grown deeper. A little later, they saw two women in a buckboard but once again they only paused and rode on.

A war party that passed up two perfectly good chances to strike. It was out of character. It didn't fit the pattern of small war parties. Curiosity made him follow, and as the dusk began to turn the last of the day into purple grayness his frown grew still deeper. The Crow didn't turn back. They continued their purposeful way, falling into single-file formation. He watched the night lower itself over the land and the Crow continued on. One more strange, out-of-character piece of behavior, he'd noted. Like most Indians, the Crow didn't like night attacks unless there was some dire need. Especially for small war parties. Yet these kept the ponies moving on through the night and he followed, being careful to stay back far enough. The almost full moon rose to let him see the column of silent riders ahead of him.

He stayed tailing them, curiosity still a part of it but there was more, now. They were no idle riders out for a moonlit canter. They spelled terror, death, destruction. They wore war paint and they had a target, someplace, somewhere, and suddenly lives were in his hands. He could spell the difference between survival and slaughter. And so he'd continued to trail the war party, hanging back under the pale moon, and he followed them into a lush valley. Halfway down, he saw them halt, slide from their ponies and settle down. He dismounted, led the Ovaro a little closer, near enough to see that the Crow had settled down to wait, not sleep. He moved a little closer and halted. Any further and they'd smell him. He settled himself against a big tanbark oak, peered down into the valley but the night let him see but a few dozen yards beyond the waiting Crow where he saw only oak and tall underbrush. He leaned his head back against the tree and the night stayed still, a waiting night.

His mouth turned down in displeasure. This was not how he had planned to spend the night, not for damn sure; he grunted inwardly. He had intended to be in Prairie Dog at this hour, in a real bed with a warm-fleshed woman. He let thoughts go back over the past forty-eight hours. He had run into a celebration when he brought the five big Owensboro California rack-bed wagons into Dustyville, each loaded down with everything from dry goods to whiskey. Dustyville lay just east of the Black Hills; damn few supply wagons were willing to risk the journey through the Sioux country and fewer made it. So his arrival with the wagons had become an instant celebration, a roaring, whiskey-flowing welcome. He'd enjoyed all of it and it was still going on when he pulled out in the morning to head north and cross the Cheyenne to Prairie Dog.

His lips turned up, formed a smile made of anticipation. Dolly was in Prairie Dog and she'd be making him welcome once she got over being surprised. Dolly had written him months back to tell him he'd be welcome anytime and to urge him to find a way to visit. The five wagons to Dustyville had given him a way and he smiled as he thought back to Dolly Westin and past years, let himself enjoy the warmth of good memories. But he snapped off remembering as he saw how far down the sky the moon had traveled. It would be dawn in another hour; he frowned, and still the Crow waited, deep shadows unmoving in the fading moonlight. Slowly, the last of the night gave way to the faint gray glow of dawn and Fargo watched the grayness take on streaks of pink, as though the sun were reluctant to come out. He half rose as the new day let the valley take shape and he saw the Indians stir, begin to rise. Fargo felt his mouth become a thin, hard line as, at the bottom of the small valley, he saw the three cabins.

He stared down the slope as the Indians began to move. Three cabins, three families trying to build a life in this untamed land, pioneers who counted on their own strengths to prevail over the savagery of nature and of the red man. They had built their homes in a loose triangle for defense, Fargo saw, each cabin able to protect the other and now he saw why the Crow had waited. They would let those in the cabins wake, come outside to fetch water from the well, stretch, greet the new day, bring in firewood for the morning coffeepot. The arrows would whistle through the air then, cut down those already outside, whether it be man, woman or child. Others would rush out, pulled by love, care, need—emotions not reason governing their reactions—and another volley of arrows would find their mark. The full attack would erupt then, but the battle already won.

He understood their waiting now, their tactics, but little else. Why these cabins? Why had they passed up easier victories? The questions remained and Fargo drew the big Sharps from its saddle holster. The Crow were on the move, flying down the slope, pulling their ponies after them. They'd be in firing range in moments and Fargo quickened his pace, found a boulder and slid to a halt. The Crow were still unaware of him, their attention focused on the three cabins. Fargo raised the rifle, saw the door of the nearest cabin start to open. The Crow froze in position, arrows on drawn bowstrings. Fargo fired, the rifle exploding the dawn stillness. Fargo saw the cabin door slam shut as one of the Crow buckled in two, pitched face forward to roll down the slope.

Fargo dropped flat as the Crow snapped around, sought him, but they turned back to the cabins. They had committed themselves to the attack and they would follow through. That was their way, even though their plans had been shattered. Fargo saw them change from stealth to fury as they swung onto their horses, raced down the slope with their screaming war cries. But he saw the rifle barrels being poked through firing holes in the cabins, exploding in gunfire, pulling back to reload. The Crow fell back on their usual tactics, racing around the three cabins while pouring arrows into them. But the three cabins in their triangle managed to return a respectable volume of cross fire, Fargo saw as he pulled himself onto the Ovaro and started to move across the slope. He reined up to aim at one fiercely riding buck, fired, and the Crow flew from his horse, seemed to hang suspended in midair as the horse charged on, dropped lifelessly in front of the center cabin.

Fargo turned as he heard the crash of glass from the cabin to the right and saw four arrows cave in the small window. The circling Crow poured another hail of arrows at once through the smashed window and Fargo turned his horse to head down the slope toward the cabins and the circling attackers. He fired the big Sharps as he streaked downward, saw a Crow catapult from his horse and saw still another take two bullets fired from the cabins, drop from his horse as though he were a sack of grain. The remaining Crow suddenly broke off the attack, veered away and started up the slope. One made only a few yards before a shot from one of the cabins brought him down.

Fargo reined up as he saw the five Crow racing toward him, focusing their rage and frustration on him, now all too aware that without his warning shot they'd have had their victory. Fargo spun the Ovaro around and started up the slope, saw the Crow veer off in two groups to flank him, two on one side, three on the other. Their tough, short-legged Indian ponies made for the steep slope; he saw they were moving too close too fast. They'd have him outflanked in moments, pour arrows at him from both sides. He could bring down some but the arrows from the other side were certain to get him. He slowed the pinto, let the Crow come up abreast of him on both flanks, bowstrings drawn when he reined up sharply and saw the first volley of arrows from both sides whistle past in front of his horse's head. He slid back across the Ovaro's rump and hit the ground, the Sharps still in one hand.

The Crow wheeled, started toward him again from both sides. He fired lying almost prone, sent the first buck flying off his pony with his upper chest caved in. The other four reined up, wheeled as Fargo fired again and another buck gave a strangled gasp, fell from his steed with one hip dangling as though he were a doll improperly put together. Fargo rolled, slid into deeper brush as he saw the remaining three Crow leap from their ponies and disappear into the high brush, and he cursed in silent rage that he hadn't been able to bring down at least one more. They were more dangerous in the high brush and he slid his way backward down the slope, halted, listened. The brush rustled above him, in a line with him, and again to his right. He stayed motionless, ears straining, smiled grimly as he caught the sound of the brush at his left.

They were moving at him from three sides, the front and both sides. Once again, they were coming in to outflank him, this time with a pincer move from the front added on. And again, he'd not be able to stay in place and get the three of them at once. He waited, listened to the brush move as they drew in. They were crawling on their bellies, staying down beneath the top line of the high brush. The one coming down from above was moving the fastest. His lips pursed as thoughts raced through his mind. They expected him to slide downhill, give way before them. The two flankers would be moving downhill to anticipate that, he knew. He glanced down along his body, drew his legs up and dug his heel into the earth, dug it in again and dislodged a clod of earth and small stones. He pushed with his foot, sent the stones tumbling down the slope through the brush. The stones clattered their way, simulating the sound he might make sliding downhill. But he didn't slide after them. Instead he pulled himself up the slope, the sound of the stones covering his movements. He pulled again, the Sharps in one hand. He stopped, heard the Indian just above and in front of him hurry his pace, lift himself to his hands and knees to do so.

Fargo was there, waiting, as the astonished Crow came through the brush, the Indian's jaw dropping open as he saw the man he didn't expect to see. The Crow never closed his jaw as Fargo fired the rifle at point-blank range. His head disappeared, simply vanished to leave a haze of droplets tinted red that rose up from the headless body. Fargo whirled, heard the other two Crow changing direction in the brush. They were scurrying away and he watched the brush move, saw them hurrying to their horses. He turned, raised the Sharps, zeroed in on the one to his left. But the Crow stayed low till he was around the far side of his horse when he vaulted onto the animal's back and lay almost flat across the horse's loins and withers as he raced away. Fargo's shot singed the Indian's long, black hair but nothing more, and he turned, saw the other Crow already galloping his pony up the slope. They had had enough and headed for a safer place.

Fargo waited till the sound of their horses was swallowed up in the new morning, rose, retrieved the Ovaro and slowly started to walk down the slope toward the cabins. He'd reached the bottom when the cabin doors opened, the men coming out first, the women close after them and the kids hanging in the open doorways, lots of kids, he noted as his glance swept the three cabins. A tall man with sideburns and a long face came toward him, hand outstretched. "We owe you, mister, all of us," he said. "Your shot saved us."

Another man, reddish hair and beard, came up. "Sneakin' savages, waitin' to bushwhack us afore our eyes was half open," he said.

"They had it planned out, all right," Fargo said. "When a Crow rides, he rides well; when he shoots, he shoots well and when he bushwhacks, he does it right, the most surprise for the least resistance."

"I'm Seth Hawkins," the tall man with the side-burns said. "This here is Jed Cranepool." He gestured to a third man, shorter, with a young, open face, who had come up. "Hiram Graney," he introduced. "And who might you be, mister?" he asked.

"Fargo ... Skye Fargo. Some folks call me the Trailsman," the big man with the lake-blue eyes answered.

Seth Hawkins nodded, his eyes taking on new respect as well as gratitude. "Heard your name back Kansas way," he said. "Those murderin' savages must've been waiting through the night for us to come out. How'd you spot them?"

"Been tailing them since north of the Cheyenne,"

Fargo said. "When I saw them pass up two Conestogas and a pair of women in a buckboard I figured they had something bigger in mind." His eyes moved over the three men and their wives who had come up to listen. "Any reason why they'd come here and single out you folks?"

"Hell, no," Seth Hawkins said. "Guess they don't need any special reason except to wipe us out."

Fargo's lips pursed. "These came special. There was a reason beyond that."

"Such as?" the settler asked.

"Don't know and can't figure it now," Fargo said. "But there was a reason. The Conestogas and the two women weren't enough for them. They wanted you."

The three men shrugged but the younger one, Hiram Graney, frowned in thought. "Things have been real quiet the last few weeks. A trapper passing through told me to be careful, said there'd been three attacks. Something's got the Indians stirred up, he said." Hiram Graney's frown deepened. "But it's got nothing to do with us. We haven't done anything to anybody. Why come after us?" he asked as much to himself as to the others.

Jed Cranepool cut in. "Fact is, it's been so quiet and peaceful, we got careless. We'd have paid hard except for you. That calls for a specially good breakfast, I'd say."

"Sounds good to me." Fargo followed the others into the center cabin. The women fixed hot biscuits, good coffee and pork sausages, and the families crowded together in the one cabin. Seth Hawkins said a prayerful grace of thanks and everyone pitched into their food. Fargo ate well, watched, listened as everyone spoke their mind, full of nervous relief at being alive. They were convinced the attack had come because they were there, with no more special reason than that. They'd done nothing to bring the attack on themselves, Fargo was convinced. They weren't lying to him, holding back. They weren't that kind. When he finally took his leave he did so hoping they were right in their convictions. But as he slowly rode out of the little valley he knew there'd been something more. It had been no random attack. Something had triggered it, made the Crow choose the three families.

He crested the slope with the nagging feeling that he'd find out why and be sorry for it.

JOIN THE TRAILSMAN READER'S PANEL
AND PREVIEW NEW BOOKS

If you're a reader of TRAILSMAN, New American Library wants to bring you more of the type of books you enjoy. For this reason we're asking you to join TRAILSMAN Reader's Panel, to preview new books, so we can learn more about your reading tastes.

Please fill out and mail today. Your comments are appreciated.

1. The title of the last paperback book I bought was: _____
   _____

2. How many paperback books have you bought for yourself in the last six months?
   ☐ 1 to 3   ☐ 4 to 6   ☐ 10 to 20   ☐ 21 or more

3. What other paperback fiction have you read in the past six months? Please list titles: _____
   _____
   _____
   _____

4. I usually buy my books at: (Check One or more)
   ☐ Book Store   ☐ Newsstand   ☐ Discount Store
   ☐ Supermarket   ☐ Drug Store   ☐ Department Store
   ☐ Other (Please specify)_____

5. I listen to radio regularly: (Check One)   ☐ Yes   ☐ No
   My favorite station is:_____
   I usually listen to radio (Circle One or more)   On way to work /
   During the day / Coming home from work / In the evening

6. I read magazines regularly: (Check One)   ☐ Yes   ☐ No
   My favorite magazine is:_____

7. I read a newspaper regularly: (Check One)   ☐ Yes   ☐ No
   My favorite newspaper is:_____
   My favorite section of the newspaper is:_____

For our records, we need this information from all our Reader's Panel Members.
NAME:_____
ADDRESS:_____ ZIP_____
TELEPHONE: Area Code (   ) Number_____

8. (Check One)   ☐ Male   ☐ Female

9. Age (Check One)   ☐ 17 and under   ☐ 18 to 34
   ☐ 35 to 49   ☐ 50 to 64   ☐ 65 and over

10. Education (Check One)
    ☐ Now in high school   ☐ Graduated high school
    ☐ Now in college   ☐ Completed some college
    ☐ Graduated college

As our special thanks to all members of our Reader's Panel, we'll send a free gift of special interest to readers of THE TRAILSMAN.

Thank you. Please mail this in today.

NEW AMERICAN LIBRARY
PROMOTION DEPARTMENT
1633 BROADWAY
NEW YORK, NY 10019